PRAISE FOR MJ JAMES

James's effective worldbuilding employs strong emotional and sensory descriptions ... often paralleling our society's own issues with neurodivergence, gender equality, economic disparity, and more.

THE BOOKLIFE PRIZE ON THE
IMMORTAL PART OF MYSELF

Good world-building and a storyline I was quickly hooked into.

GOODREADS REVIEWER ON IN-
BETWEEN

BIRK

EMBER TOWN SERIES
BOOK 3

MJ JAMES

Editor services provided by Rebecca Scharpf at Scrollwork Edits

Proofreading editor services provided by Skey Alley

Cover design by MJ James

ebook ISBN: 978-1-958175-19-4

paperback ISBN: 978-1-958175-22-4

audiobook ISBN: 978-1-958175-23-1

TRIGGER WARNING

I believe that there is good in the world. I also know that the road to joy, especially for queer people, is not one without bumps. I write about queer and neurodiverse joy, but with that joy comes those who feel threatened by our joy. A part of me hopes that by mirroring other's actions, they can understand why what they do is hurtful. However unlikely that may be, I do know that my readers deal with ignorant and hateful comments nearly every day. As always, there are no hard feelings if you need to walk away.

Birk Contains
Transphobia
Deadnaming (censored)
Misgendering (censored as the MC transitions)
Family Dissownment
TERF Representation
Light physical actions on the page (i.e., kissing)

ALSO BY MJ JAMES

In-Between

The Immortal Part of Myself

NeurodiVeRse

The Ember Town Series

Lucas

Phoenix

Birk

Mika

The council room was fuller than normal with people packed so close that everyone was touching. The air was stuffy and full of tension. Birk hadn't even wanted to be at the council meeting. They had other, more important, things on their mind. However, Elowen, their mother, had insisted they attend. Birk knew she didn't want to be grand-standed by the alpha and his daughter, who had taken down Veronica. The story had already spread across the magical community, but Birk had heard it from Lucas. It wasn't precisely a firsthand account, but it was as close as they could expect.

Lucas wasn't permitted outside the Ranch, but the vampires seemed willing enough to allow Birk to visit as long as they didn't overstay their welcome. It helped that the vampires said that nymphs smelled more like trees than anything resembling humans, a compliment Birk was willing to take. They held on to the words Lucas had given them during their first brief encounter. The ones that had helped them start understanding who they were. They were non-binary. They were also a nymph—so at least one nymph was not female.

Birk could feel their tree, even here in this crowded room. Part of them was in the forest. Their tall, slender silver birch, from which they had taken their new name, had been planted right after their birth. They had been connected, and their tree now contained their soul. It was there, settled in the forest, just waiting for their return.

Birk felt the jostling of those around them, bringing their attention back to the meeting. The alpha's daughter was busy kicking her cousin out. Part of Birk was relieved at the outcome. They had never much liked Jared; he was always swaggering around like he owned the place but then acted stupider than a beetle.

"That turned out well. I'm glad there will finally be a woman as leader of the wolf pack and the council. It is about time were given our proper respect. With so many men around making decisions, it is no wonder things have been getting all screwed up. Now, how about we head back?" Birk let their mother ramble on. Her distaste for everyone who was not herself was familiar, even if it consistently made Birk uncomfortable. One day, they would have to tell their mother who they really were, but the thought left them confused and scared. Their soul stood next to their sisters, but they knew their mother would not accept them for who they were. As far as she was concerned, anyone who wasn't female was less, and anyone who was a nymph was female. Maybe their mother couldn't send them to the river like all of their sons, but there was a good chance she would try.

The crowds started to shift as the meeting reached its

dramatic conclusion. Suddenly, they stumbled as a body slammed into their own.

"I'm sorry. I'm not sure how that happened. Everyone seems to be overly excited today." It was a vampire Birk vaguely recognized, although they couldn't place him.

"Oh, I know you," the stranger said. "My partner Lucas met you out by the river."

"I think you must be mistaken," Birk said.

"Do you mean the one who chose to be a man?" Birk's mother asked.

"Now, hey, no need to talk like that. He didn't choose anything except to be who he is. I think you may understand a thing or two about that."

"What do you mean by that?" The older nymph asked.

"I think I made a mistake. I'm so sorry." He gave Birk an apologetic look, but it was too late. "I was putting my foot in my mouth. It is kind of my thing. Don't worry nothing about what I said." He turned to the older nymph. "Ma'am." Then he turned to the younger nymph. "Birk, if you ever need anything, just let Lucas and me know."

He left then, but the damage had already been done.

"What term of respect is 'Birk'? Why would he think you would ever need his help—a *man's* help? A *vampire man's* help."

Birk let her ramble on, hoping that, in her disgust, she would forget to question the situation. But she didn't. She stopped and looked at them, expecting some sort of response.

"Birk is … well … it is my name … that I use … sometimes."

"And why would you need a new name?"

Her mother put her hand on their elbow and started

pulling Birk out of the council room. They considered breaking free and running, but where would they go? Their tree was still in the forest under their mother's control.

"Why would you go around using this silly name instead of J— the perfectly respectable name I gave you? It was a name handed down through our family line since the start, long before the humans even evolved. We should have wiped them out before they could evolve, but now there are too many. We must protect our trees before they cut them down like so many others."

This time, their mother didn't seem to need a response. She continued dragging them toward their car, an electric one they only used when it couldn't be avoided—like for council meetings. Birk strapped in, tuning out their mother's latest rant about the evils of cars, and waited until they could return to the forest. Hopefully their mother would forget everything that had happened over the course of the night.

It was early morning as they headed back to the forest. The sun was still a few hours from rising, and the road was baren. Most of the humans were still tucked up in their houses, hidden away from the darkness.

Birk watched the trees fly past as they drove. They were shadows highlighted briefly by their headlights. Those nearest the road must have been used to the intrusion, but they couldn't help but wonder if, given the choice, they would uproot and find a quieter part of land on which to grow.

The ride had been silent; their mother had stopped ranting once they had closed their doors. When you lived for over a century, cars were still considered new inventions, and the speeds at which they traveled were unnatural. At least, that was what their mother had constantly told them. Birk, on the other hand, enjoyed the peace car rides offered.

They parked in a gravel lot not far from their forest. It was one of the few concessions of modernity Birk's mother had given in to. Off the parking lot there was a trail that led to their home, a magical path hidden from all those who did not belong. It was not hidden from Birk, who had been born into the nymph magic, another sign that their gender didn't stop them from being a nymph. At the end of the path they found their sisters, asleep on the grass or wherever they found comfort. A few went home to their trees each night, sleeping nestled in their roots, something Birk had fantasized about for the last few hours. They hoped for at least a little rest before the sun appeared and the sisterhood awoke.

"I think I'll just—" Birk started to say, but one look from their mother stopped them.

"The night is almost over; don't waste time walking to your tree. Stay with your sisters. Remember who you are." Then she strode away and lay down beside a trio of women nestled together. They shifted in their sleep, making room for their leader, almost as if they merged into one.

Birk looked longingly in the direction of their tree. Their mother expected her word to be followed absolutely, enough that she didn't even think to wait to see if her child obeyed her. *No one* disobeyed her; the consequences were never worth it in the end. Birk hoped they would be able to sleep with their tree tomorrow. They needed to feel the texture of its bark underneath their fingers and the comfort of knowing they belonged somewhere.

Birk found a pine tree, one that only held its own soul, and sat down beside it. They could still see their sisters. They would know that they were there throughout the night, but they were far enough away to pretend, for a few moments, that they had privacy—something they hadn't experienced since college.

By the time the sun started peeking through the branches, most of the women had already awoken. Birk got up, stretching their limbs. It felt like they had barely slept at all, and from their watch, hidden carefully under their long-sleeved T-shirt, it had been less than three hours. Nymphs might not have the same physical needs as humans, but they did need more than three hours of sleep a night—not that you could tell that from their mother. Elowen was already awake, sitting next to a group of women eating a breakfast of foraged roots and dried berries.

The nymphs lived off the land, just like their trees. They were caregivers, taking only what they needed and giving back even more. Occasionally, during special events, they would include a feast with meat, but more often than not, it consisted of whatever they had foraged.

Birk knew that they were lucky. While they had never met another group of nymphs, they had studied their regions, and Colorado was home to one of the few families that did not have to barter to sustain themselves. Not that

Birk wouldn't mind bartering. They picked up a handful of breakfast, and their mind returned to their first taste of pizza—the greasy cheese that had filled their mouth. They had thrown up for a week, their stomach not having tasted anything like it before—it had been worth it. They had gotten a taste for the outside world that had followed them home. A few places in town were run by magicals and would hook them up, knowing they didn't have money. But it had been too long since they had been allowed out alone.

After Birk swallowed their handful of nuts and berries, they strode briskly, sidestepping the women waiting for their daily assignments, determined to reach their mother.

"I was thinking today would be a good day to head into town and get the feel of things after what happened last night," they said.

"Your place is here." Elowen didn't even turn to address Birk when she spoke. "You will go out with Sister Woodruff to clean up the river. The human garbage has overrun it once again."

"I thought it was my place to connect to other species and advocate for our people. Isn't that why you sent me away to get an education? Yet all you do is keep me here with our sisters."

"All that matters is here." She turned, her eyes bright as she spoke. "We have our people and our land. They will be with you far longer than anything you find in the outside world. Is cleaning the river not important?"

"It is important, I just …"

"Good. Then go. When you are back, I have something I want to discuss with you."

"Come on, Sister J—," Sister Woodruff said.

Birk cringed at the use of their birth name, the name that

connected them to an identity that wasn't their own. They didn't know how to unite who they were with who their family thought they were, so they dutifully followed the older woman out of the clearing and to the small storage shed by the parking lot.

They pulled out the yellow vests, track sticks, sashes, and garbage bags and started the hike toward the river.

They worked the morning in silence, moving their way down one side of the river until they reached the edge of their territory. It was a weekly chore, and despite what their mother believed, most of the humans in Ember were respectful of the nature around them. There were one too many scary stories told around campfires about people who disrespected the land. Between them, they only had a satchel full of dead wood and a small amount of trash. They combined their trash into one bag and left it tied to a branch in one of the trees. A local ranger knew to come and pick it up.

The journey had only taken them a few hours, and it was nearing lunchtime. They were not far from the road, and Birk was confident they could get a ride back into town. Enough people knew them, even the humans, to feel comfortable picking them up.

"I wouldn't do that if I were you." The older woman eyed Birk as she spoke.

"Do what?"

"Your mother just cares about you. She cares about all of us."

"She wouldn't even notice. She has experienced too much time to care about a few hours. You could come into town with me and visit the man you had your eye on. I'm sure that he wouldn't mind seeing you again."

Woodruff smiled at that, and Birk thought that perhaps they would get their way this time, but the older woman became serious again.

"Your mother is concerned. She wouldn't like you going back into town. She may have lived many years, but you are the only daughter she has. J—, she just wants to protect you."

"I'm not, though." Birk let out a deep sigh and, defeated, started walking back toward their home.

"What do you mean?" The older woman fell in beside them.

"Nothing. But you promised to call me Birk when she wasn't around. Please."

"Changing your name won't change your responsibilities."

"I'm not even allowed to perform my responsibilities. I am supposed to serve as a connection outside our family, but beyond the four years of college, I have never been allowed to leave. I have never even seen another nymph family. Why won't she let us see our sisters?"

"It is just how it is done. She makes these decisions for our own good. Now, let's hurry back while there is still some lunch left."

Their home was an open field. It was in a place that was both very real and yet held apart by magic. Birk had been taught that it was a natural occurrence when more than one of their kind joined together in a family, allowing them a safe place to live near their trees so they could protect them, just like the trees protected their souls. But there were no trees in the clearing itself, just lush green grass and a view straight up to the sky.

The clearing also had a freshwater lake from which they gathered water. They used it to drink and bathe, but there was no lake in Ember. There was only the river that ran through town. At one point, Birk had questioned how their home worked. Now, they knew it was the land providing for their family's needs.

The clearing's floor was covered in soft vibrant green grass that made for comfortable sleeping. Creatures would wander in and share the space with the women, but the insects did not bother them any more than the nymphs disrupted their homes.

If it weren't for the chattering of all the women, it would

be a tranquil place. There were several hundred nymphs that lived together in their family—one of the largest families left, led by her mother for the last few centuries. Their family history connected them to the land for several hundred generations. They were the first settlers of Ember, coming into being at the same time as the trees. Or so Birk had been taught.

They had changed over the years as the women had bred with the men who had come near their family. While most of the women had a deep brown skin tone, there were those with ebony tones, some who had Asian ancestors, and even those with skin so pale you could almost see through it. Birk had thought such diversity was normal until they had gone away to university and learned the history of humans. Part of them understood why their mother kept them hidden away as much as possible. But a deeper part longed to stretch their roots. Nymphs were not meant to travel, but sometimes, when the dirt had been sucked dry of all nutrients, trees needed to be planted somewhere else.

There was no room for change here, no way for this group to accept them for who they were, at least not unless their mother gave them permission. Birk was expected to join them, to fill the rest of their days with the companionship of the same women they had known their whole life—the same women who still saw them as the leader's daughter.

So, they did what they always did. Birk went to the edge of the clearing, where the trees huddled close. There, they found their bag, a simple backpack left over from their college days, that held their possessions.

There was nothing specifically against nymphs owning

things. It was more that no one had thought to own things. Everything belonged to the community; all you needed was clothing, if you chose to wear it, and the tools you needed to do your chores. But Birk found they couldn't let everything go, and managed to bring their bag in with a few items from college. It held some of their favorite books and a journal full of blank pages because they were too afraid to write down their thoughts.

They pulled out *Silent Spring*, flipped to a random page, and started reading.

They felt it when their mother started to approach them. They were connected—not like they were connected to their tree, like part of the same whole, but a part of them fit together, just like every sister in the family. When they had gone away to school, they had felt that loss, and it was a loss, although, it had not tugged at them in the same way the loss of their tree had. Still, Birk had thought coming home would help make them feel whole. Instead, they felt like they were losing more of themself day after day. It had been a decade, and nothing had felt more real than those four years away.

Before their mother had made it past the first line of trees, Birk had their book packed away and rounded the trunk to greet her. While possessions weren't forbidden, it also wasn't best to advertise them.

"Come, it's time to talk," their mother said. Then she walked away, once again full of certainty Birk would follow.

Birk looked around for any other option and then trailed after their mother.

"Okay, let's talk," Birk said.

They stood at the edge of the trees, away from the clearing, but Birk could see the nymphs gathering together, most likely at their mother's behest. The last thing Birk wanted was to go back among the women and pretend to be someone they were not.

"Not here," their mother said. "We need to return to our sisters."

"Why?"

Disbelief flashed across her face. No one stood up to her, no matter how trivial her demand was. Birk thought that it was probably past time that someone did. Instead of responding, their mother just started walking, once again expecting to be followed.

"I'm not going back there. If you want to talk to me, we can do it out here, away from the others."

Their mother just kept walking. Birk stood there debating the consequences of not following. They could ignore her and go back and sit down with their book for the rest of the night. They would miss dinner, but it would be a good price to pay for not participating in the drama their mother was currently performing. However, before walking too far away, their mother turned back around.

"I guess I will just tell everyone you refused the summons."

"An official summons?"

Their mother stared at them expectantly, watching the disbelief and then uncertainty flash across their face. Official summonses were reserved for family business. Everyone who was away was called back and expected to attend. Granted, that wasn't very hard. The few people who went away were only gone for a few years for college or occasionally stayed away long enough to give birth before returning, and even that was not common. There was only one nymph currently away, and she attended a school in Denver. They had probably waited until she had arrived to start the meeting. With very little choice, Birk started walking, catching up to their mother.

"What is this about?"

"Don't worry, baby bird. You wouldn't want to ruin the surprise."

Birk's insides twisted at the use of the nickname. Whatever was happening wouldn't be pleasant.

When they arrived at the clearing, the women parted to let them through. They were at the gathering site, a small hill surrounded by a lush grass field. As Birk and their mother went up the hill, the women began to sit down, getting comfortable in the grass. Nymphs were not one to stand at attention, and while they did any work needed without complaint, they were also the first ones to enjoy long periods of rest without any qualms. Birk had seemed to be born without this ability, instead having always been prone to worry and anxiety. They had known they were different from a young age, even if they hadn't known why at the time.

"Hello, my sisters," Birk's mother welcomed them. The nymphs clapped and squealed in delight. It seemed child-like, but that was only if Birk judged it based on the human perceptions they had picked up. The ability to feel joy was one of the nymphs' greatest strengths. "Thank you for coming to the summons."

Birk looked out at their family. The sea of women were primarily naked or dressed in white garb that covered small portions of their bodies and were accentuated with dyed fabric. The younger nymphs, like Birk, were clothed in more human attire. Ash was dressed like a typical college student in blue jeans and a T-shirt. It would blend in easily on campus, but it made her stick out here. The few younger children were mostly in simple, bright cotton dresses that had been picked up and traded through the family as the children had grown. Even the baby was in a white human onesie.

Nymphs didn't propagate fast. They had to leave the family to find a mate and then return to raise the child. For most, it was a harrowing journey, combined with the knowledge that if their child were born male, they would have to watch it given to the river. Female partnerships within the family were the norm. Two or more women grouped for a time before separating and finding other pair-ings. It kept their family from growing fast, but considering how long they lived, it worked for them.

Birk studied the people surrounding them. These were the people who had helped raise them, and they had known from a young age that one day, they would be expected to lead them. Birk had seen the younger ones born or returned as infants. They had known them their entire lives. This was all Birk had known, but as their mother dragged them to the center of the gathering, they knew deep within themself that they no longer belonged. Only women were allowed to be nymphs, and Birk was not a woman.

"Today is a special day," Elowen said. "Today is the day I step down as your matron."

There was a collective gasp and then silence for a few heartbeats while everyone processed what had been said. Birk stood still, certain this was another gimmick of their mother's.

"What does this mean?"

"Who will lead us?"

"No, no, no."

The voices rang out at the same time, making it impossible to know who was saying what. More questions blended together until the sisterhood became a choir of squawking birds, each voice droning together until nothing was distinguishable.

Elowen let them talk, building up the drama of her announcement until she raised her hands above her head, calling for silence.

"Sisters … sisters … SISTERS." They quieted down enough for Elowen's voice to rise above their murmurings. "You have seen how the tide is changing in the magical community. The mantle of leadership has been handed down to the new generation, a generation more apt at dealing with all the change. It is time for my daughter, our sister J— to lead the family."

"We can't lose you!" The call came from one of the older

nymphs who had already birthed two children and raised one of them.

"Do not worry, my sisters. I will still be here helping her make the correct decisions. It is necessary to guide the youth; I will not let her lead you astray."

Birk stood frozen before their family. They had expected their mother to pull a stunt, but not this. Faces strained up at them. A few were friendly, like Sister Woodruff's. However, most showed concern. They had all paused, as if waiting for them to say something.

"You want me to lead the sisterhood?"

"With my help, of course," their mother said.

"Why?"

The clearing had gone quiet, and all the sisters leaned forward. Birk knew they should never question their mother, especially with everyone listening. However, this was all too much, too fast.

"Why?" their mother repeated. "Isn't it enough that I have said so?"

"If I am to be matron, then it does matter. I need to understand, or I will not be able to lead."

"You don't need to worry about making decisions. I will be here to help you with that. You will be a fresh face for the council meetings, but I will prep you beforehand so you know what to say. It might be best if I also attend with you for a while."

"So you are installing me as a figurehead. I won't be able to make any changes?" Birk faced their mother, trying to ignore the hundreds of eyes watching.

"Changes? What kind of changes do you want to make? Everything functions perfectly."

"Well, how about only having female nymphs? Shouldn't we at least let the sons be raised alongside us, even if they can't be nymphs?"

The crowd froze. Any movement ceased. The sudden stillness pierced into Birk, and they almost regretted asking, but they had to know. If they were going to lead, they would have to do it as themself, and while they weren't male, they weren't female either. It had seemed like a cautious place to start. Except now, it didn't seem so safe.

Birk looked at their mother, whose eyes seemed to have grown in size. Her fists were clenched, and her lips were pinched together. After the silence had become so thick that it had taken on a persona all its own, their mother finally spoke, their words projecting throughout the entire territory.

"Men are not welcome here. This space is for our sister-hood. How dare you defile it with a suggestion that appalling. How did you even get such an idea into your head?"

"I am not a sister. I am not male or female. I am agender, meaning I am neither, and yet still have a tree. I am a nymph. If you cannot accept boys to be raised beside us, how can you accept me as I am?" The words just slipped out. Birk had not wanted them said this way, in front of this many people. But now that they were out, they felt a little lighter, at least until their mother's reply.

"I cannot."

Birk wobbled on their feet and disconnected from the world as their mother continued speaking.

"I have known others like yourself. It is an illness. That vampire brought this into our land, and you must allow us to help heal you. You must work extra hard to hold on to your femininity. To be a woman is a gift that should not be denied. We will help heal you."

"I'm not sick. This isn't something new. I have known I am different from you for years. You all have known it as well." The crowd started looking anywhere but at the mother and child, afraid to be brought into the conversation. "I finally have the language to tell you who I am. I am agender and I am a nymph."

"Get out." The words echoed through the group.

Birk stood frozen, trying to process what their mother had said.

"I said, get out. Do not come back until you are willing to be the daughter I created."

Birk started walking then, their legs aware of what they needed to do even if their mind hadn't entirely caught up to what was happening. They found themself at the edge of the clearing where they had left their bag, and they picked it up before continuing.

They were not surprised to find themself at their tree. It was a tall gray birk tree, also known as a silver birch. When they were younger, they had climbed among its slender branches, spending days at a time sustained only by the energy it created. Now that they were older, they could no longer climb their tree. Its energy was now only enough to sustain their soul, not their adult-sized physical form.

Birk sat down against its trunk, grateful for their old friend. Tears started to flow then, as their mind questioned why they had chosen that moment to come out to everyone all at once. At the same time, they felt like they had been forced into a corner, asked to choose between their family and their identity. It had likely been their mother's plan, although they doubted it had gone the way she had expected.

Tears flowed freely, watering their tree, but silently enough so their sisters could not hear.

Birk awoke to the feel of bare feet kicking into their thigh. They reached down to rub away the pain, trying to remember where they were. Their face was crusty, and their back hurt from sleeping at an awkward angle. Before the night's events rushed back at them, a second kick landed against their hand so hard that one of their fingers popped.

When they opened their eyes, they were not surprised to see their mother standing over them.

"I thought I told you to leave."

Birk held their finger with their other hand, wincing as they popped it back into place. There was no doctor in the sisterhood. They all had to help each other when needed. Birk put off answering their mother as long as they dared.

"I did what you said. I left."

"This is still my land. You have no right to be here."

"This is my tree." Birk stood up as they spoke. "I have every right to be here."

"Your tree? So you are already ready to take back what you said last night. Well then, let's go back and tell everyone it was a misunderstanding." Elowen grabbed them by their arm and started pulling.

"There was no misunderstanding." Birk jerked away from their mother, then took a few steps back. "I am not female. But even you cannot deny that I am a nymph. I was bonded to a tree on my first birthday. Here it has been growing ever since, holding my soul. How am I not a nymph?"

Faster than Birk could react, their mother moved forward and pushed them back down.

"Get out. No daughter of mine will deny their femininity. It is a right and a privilege, and your declaration hurts us all."

"How? I haven't said females and femininity do not exist. I have just said that those terms do not describe *me*. I wish to remain with my sisters, as I truly am."

"You have been asked to vacate my land. If you step foot back on it before issuing an apology, you will forfeit your tree and, as such, your soul."

Birk had thought they had lost everything last night, but now they found they had more to lose. To be separated from one's soul was the worst punishment that could be bestowed upon a nymph. Birk had only heard of one other who had received the punishment long before she had been born. One sister had been upset at another and brought her harm by carving deep gashes into her tree that could still be seen to this day. Birk had visited both trees in their youth. Sister Marie's tree was marred by slashes. Since the incident, she had spent her days with a distant look in her eye as she had been cared for by others. Birk had never heard her speak. The second tree was whole but tied with a blue ribbon that had faded with age. It was a mark given to those who were condemned to death before death—those banished to wander the world without access to their soul. As a child, the older sisters would tell this story late at night to scare the children.

Now, Birk was being condemned to the same fate, all because they refused to play pretend any longer. Without saying another word, Birk picked up their backpack and started walking out of the forest toward the main road.

As Birk walked down the road, they thought back to a decade ago when their mother had first come to them and told them that they had to leave the family.

"You will go and study so you can bring that knowledge back."

Birk had never gone to school. Their childhood had been spent lying on the grass, swimming in the lake, and foraging in the forest. Sister Woodruff had taught them to identify everything safe to eat, how to read, and the basics of mathematics. They had learned about the other magical communities and humans, but only through the stories their sisters had told. Birk had been sheltered and protected until their seventeenth year, and then, still a child, they had been thrust out into the world.

Their mother had not driven them into town. They had walked, just as they were doing now. They had carried a bag full of paper their mother had assured them they would need. One was for a bus ticket to their new school. The other, more colorful pieces, were for something called money.

The first time a car passed them on the road, they jumped into the forest and cried. When they reached town, they stood in amazement at the buildings and the mass of people until a man, the first man they had ever met, took pity on them and helped them find their way to the bus stop. When the metal contraption arrived, they were petrified of entering its gaping mouth. The only thing that scared them more was returning to their mother a failure. So they entered the bus and headed off to school.

This trip was not quite the same. The city was familiar, and they no longer jumped in fright when the cars drove past, although they did walk to the side near the tree line to keep from their sight. Birk could have asked for a ride, but it took everything they had to keep moving forward, away from their tree.

When Birk first arrived in Denver, the distance from their tree felt like they were being ripped in two. That on top of being dropped into a world that they did not understand. It had taken a very flustered upperclassman volunteer to show Birk to their room and explain that this was where they would live ... inside ... not out on the open lawn.

That first night, Birk cried nonstop. Finally, their roommate fetched the resident assistant, who had finally called on the faculty resident. Thankfully, she was a witch who had taken Birk under her wing. She had taught Birk everything about the human world that they needed to know, everything their mother should have taught them long before they had stepped into college.

When Birk arrived home, they made sure to take each girl to the city at least twice. Once when they were young and the sight was still masked in the wonder of childhood.

Then, the second time, before they reached adulthood. They taught the girls everything they could about how things worked in the human world. If anyone was sent off to college, Birk went with them to make sure they settled in, teaching them what they could about the world they were entering. Most didn't last more than a few weeks, but at least Birk had prepared them the best they could.

Now, their sisters would have no one.

At least when Birk went away to college, they had known they would be returning. They cried silent tears thinking about their tree, and when it became too much, they slipped away and visited.

Now, they couldn't risk it. If they were found out, they had no doubt their mother would follow up on her threat to destroy their tree, which would destroy Birk. Once again, they had to figure out how to survive.

It was completely dark by the time Birk ended up on the outskirts of town. The road had quieted down, with very few cars to worry about. They walked slowly, uncertain what their next move should be.

They thought briefly of making their way over to the Ranch and finding Lucas, maybe beseeching the Vampire Mistress to take them in. The thought of living with the creatures of the night gave them pause. They had been attending meetings with them for years, but they did not know anything about them. It was Jeffery who had put a stop to that flight of fancy. Birk knew he hadn't meant anything by outing them, but intentional or not, he had done so. Birk couldn't handle facing him now.

Instead, they kept walking. They didn't have super hearing or other magical abilities to help in a situation like this. They were a child of nature and they were stronger in the wild surrounded by the forest. But here in the city, they felt small and fragile, more so than they had in the past.

They tried to think of someplace open at this hour and could only come up with one place. There was a bar in the middle of town run by a rock troll and frequented by much of the magical community. They had never gone, never been allowed that much freedom to go. Now seemed like the perfect time to visit. They had some cash in their bag, not a lot, just some they had collected. Mostly, on previous visits, they had made connections in the town. They were places they could visit quickly, where they had helped out with their plants or other small favors, and in return had been gifted human food or books. Perhaps they could visit one of their connections in the morning and ask for help. It would be more than they had given in the past, but it was the only plan they had, as thin as it was. So they kept walking, hoping to find a place to stay until morning.

Birk worried they would not be able to find the bar, but it was easy to spot in the late hours. It was the only place open. Lights flooded the sidewalk, the muffled sound of conversation and music filtering through the windows. The door was solid oak, put together from multiple trees from areas that were not local. They paused, letting their hand linger on the wood. It was no longer alive, but they couldn't help but say a blessing of thanks before they grabbed the handle and opened the door.

The sound was louder now, and they paused on the boundary, taking in the room. A group of pixies hung around a couple of tables in the corner near a dart board, and a few werewolves played pool nearby. The wolves were a young group of mixed genders. Birk didn't recognize any of them. There were other species in pairs or by themselves at the bar, including some humans Birk had never seen before.

All the tables were taken, and the floor was full of people. The bar was packed as well, but there was one stool open. Birk headed toward it.

They sat down in between two humans and waited until the bartender came around to them.

"What will you have?" he asked. A faint whiff of the ocean accompanied his words.

Birk stared at him. He was a selkie—a selkie in Ember. Selkies did not live in small mountain towns where the closest body of water was a river ruled by merpeople. They lived in the ocean. There was a family of selkies in Northern California, but to see one behind a bar far away from his family was so shocking that they forgot how to speak for a second.

"I'm sorry," they finally managed. "Can I have whatever is cheapest?"

He picked up a cup, placed it under a tap, and pulled a lever. The amber liquid filled the cup, and he handed it over. Birk thought about the bills in their bag, hoping they had enough to cover their check.

They took a small sip and nearly spat the liquid back out again. It was bitter, with a hit of earth mixed in. Birk had only occasionally tried alcohol in college, and never beer. They took a second sip, more tentatively this time, and let the liquid go down their throat. It wasn't exactly pleasant, but it would do.

They held on to their mug throughout the night. Their bag stayed on the floor, between their feet. They stared down at the liquid, trying to ignore that the room was emptying out as the sun began to rise. When they took their last sip, they looked up and realized that there was only one other person in the room. He was a solid guy with a face that put a person at ease despite his bulk. This had to be Rocko.

"Are you closing?" they asked.

"Nah, we closed up an hour ago."

"Oh." Birk shot up, grabbing their bag. They rummaged through it and placed a few crumpled one-dollar bills on the counter. "Is this enough?"

"You're Elowen's daughter?"

"No. I mean, she is my mother, but I'm not her …" Birk trailed off, uncertain how to continue.

"I'm sorry. I misspoke: you are Elowen's child?"

Birk nodded, and when Rocko didn't respond, they slipped their bag on their shoulder and turned to go toward the door.

"Thank you," they called as they walked away.

"Do you have any place to go?" The words hit them as they reached the door, and before they knew what was happening, the stress of the day mixed with the alcohol, and they collapsed on the floor, tears running down their face. Rocko's arms wrapped around them as he helped them off the floor and into one of the table chairs.

Rocko left them as he went behind the bar and returned with a glass of water. Birk took the glass gratefully and swallowed half of it before setting it back down.

"I have a friend whom you might know," Rocko said.

Birk looked up in confusion. They didn't have many friends and weren't certain which of the ones they did know would be connected to Rocko.

"Before Tim started working here."

"Tim?" Birk interrupted.

"I'm sure you met him earlier."

"The selkie?"

Rocko nodded. "Before Tim, I had another bartender named Lucas. Unfortunately, he can't work here anymore because he was turned into a vampire. But before that, he was a human who moved here to start over in a place which would know him for who he truly was."

"You know Lucas?" Birk looked up expectantly.

"We are good friends. Since they don't let him leave the safety of the vampire community, they give me special permission to visit him now and then. He told me a story about a friend he met, a nymph, and asked me to keep an eye out if I ever saw they needed some help."

"He talked to you about me?" Birk began tracing the outside of the table with their fingers.

"Nothing specific, not even your name."

"Lucas told Jeffery, and Jeffery mentioned it to my mom."

"I see that didn't go over well."

"She banished me. She said I'm not a nymph, and I'm not allowed near my tree unless I continue pretending to be a woman. But I can't do it, not anymore. Why must nymphs be women?"

"I haven't always lived in Ember. My family lived in the desert, where the rocks run red with iron. There are no nymphs near there, but there are stories of other families."

"Have you met any of them?"

"I have not. I don't know what is true of all families. All I know is that gender is not an absolute. I have a room upstairs. I don't use it much. You are welcome to use it for tonight."

"Are you sure it's okay? I don't want to take you out of your space."

"This bar is my place. I keep the upstairs apartment around for the humans so they don't ask too many questions, but I have no need of it myself."

"Is it for the same reason you don't ever eat the food you make and why you never sleep?"

"Exactly. Would you like to use it?"

"Yes, thank you." Relief flooded through Birk, and the weight that had been on them since they had been forced out of their home lessened just slightly.

The room was just over the bar. It consisted of a small kitchen, a table, a single bed, and a bathroom. It had been years since Birk had last slept on a bed. They touched it tentatively, watching as their fingers sunk into the soft mattress. Then they caught sight of the dirt across their hands, and their mind wandered to the shower, warm water spraying from a pipe. It was something that they missed every time they went to the river to bathe. As they relaxed under the hot water and then slipped under the covers, with only their underclothes, to not dirty the sheets, they started to wonder if maybe their mother was right: they were not really a nymph because they enjoyed human comforts too much. But as they started to fall asleep, they felt the pull of their tree miles away, completely unreachable, and knew that their mother was wrong.

Birk woke to the sound of voices below them. They tried to gauge the time, but there wasn't a window in the room, and they couldn't find a single clock. After tugging on their jeans and T-shirt, they brushed off any lingering dirt and went to grab their bag but decided to leave it on the chair. They could snag it after they figured out what they were going to do.

The bar wasn't very crowded. Tim stood behind the counter, and Rocko was in the kitchen cooking something that smelled good. The pixies occupied the same seats they had claimed the day before. The only other person in the bar was a witch who was eating a sandwich and nursing a beer.

Birk recognized her instantly. She was set to lead the witch coven, but something was preventing her from taking over completely. There was gossip all over the council, but no one really talked to Birk, nor would they care to listen to gossip. Whatever was going on, it was no one's secret but her own.

"Oh good, you're up," Rocko said as he headed out of

the kitchen with a plate full of steamed vegetables and rice. He placed the plate on the table and indicated for Birk to sit. "I wasn't sure what your favorite food was, but if this doesn't work, let me know and I can fix something else up."

"This is perfect, thank you."

Rocko hovered as they picked up the fork and took their first bite. The vegetables were warm, with a slightly soft texture but enough crunch so they were not limp. They were coated in oil and seasonings, and the taste was so amazing that Birk could not help the sigh that escaped them. Even in their time away or their encounters in the city, they had never tasted anything so good. They dug in with gusto, only realizing that they needed to watch their eating habits when they heard Rocko laugh.

"Well, I'm glad that you enjoy it. Tim, can you get them something to drink, nothing with alcohol or dairy? Maybe a sparkling water."

When Birk had finished the plate, they looked up to see a glass of bubbly water by their elbow. They took a tentative sip, and the flavor of berries burst on their tongue. They looked in the glass to see where the fruit was, but they decided they didn't care and drank the water down.

With their meal done, they leaned back, more satisfied than they could remember, and caught the witch staring at them.

Birk stood up and walked over to her.

"Hi, I'm Birk," they said.

"Mika," the witch said, her eyes never once leaving Birk's face.

"Can I sit?"

When Mika didn't respond, Birk took a chance and sat

in the extra seat. "This is a pretty great place. Do you come here often?"

"Every now and then. I haven't seen you here before." Mika spoke with a clipped, no-nonsense voice.

"This is my first time, or last night was. It was the only place open … well, when I had nowhere else to go. Rocko, let me sleep upstairs."

Mika's eyes widened, but she didn't say anything.

"Is it unusual for Rocko to help someone out?"

"No, not at all. That is a big part of who he is and why he has this bar. But you must have done something to earn his trust fast for him to allow you upstairs."

Birk shrugged, uncertain what to say. "I think maybe he just felt sorry for me. I had nowhere else to go."

"If something happened to your forest, I can make some calls and get people together. We can save as many trees as possible." Mika stood, pulled a cell phone from her pocket, and was already typing before she finished her sentence.

"No." Birk rose and reached out, touching Mika's hand before they thought better of it and pulled their hand back. Her skin was soft and cool, and Birk could still feel where they had touched them. "Sorry, I just mean the trees are fine. My sisters are fine. It is just that I'm no longer allowed there."

"Oh." Mika slipped her phone in her pocket and sat back down as quickly as she'd jumped to her feet. "I'm sorry to hear that. Family can be tough."

Birk could see Mika's interest on her face, and they appreciated them not coming out and asking what had happened. But if they were going to start making connections, they needed to tell someone, and what better person to tell than someone related to the council who was dealing with her own messy drama?

"It's kind of complicated," Birk began.

"You don't need to tell me," Mika said. "If you want to, you can, but you don't need to."

"Thank you," Birk said. "I have been questioning myself from a very young age. I knew I wasn't like my sisters, but I didn't know what exactly that meant. Then a vampire came and visited my family."

"Lucas," Mika practically growled.

"You know him?"

"He used to work with Rocko behind the bar before Tim. He seems to be the catalyst of a lot of stories."

"Oh." Birk paused, and when Mika didn't say more, continued with their story. "When Lucas came to visit, I asked him some questions, and he pointed me toward further research. I'm not a woman."

"You're a trans man, like Lucas?"

"No—well, partially. I'm not a man. I know that. But I do think I am trans. I am not a woman or a man. I'm agender. My mother found out, and when I wouldn't pretend any longer, I ended up without a home."

"You are neither?" Mika asked.

"Yes. I've read as much as possible since talking to Lucas, and I've learned a lot. Some people are both male and female at the same time. Others are male at one time and female at another. I have never been either. It is why I don't feel like my sisters."

"I'm sorry," Mika said. She stood up so fast that her chair tipped slightly, and before it had righted itself, Mika was opening the door. "I'm sorry."

Birk sat staring at the empty chair. Tears welled up in the corners of their eyes. That was the second person who had left them in as many days.

The bar was still calm when Birk arrived. They had returned early from helping paint a house. Rocko had connected them to a witch named Matt, who ran a painting company. He was short-staffed, his son was off at college, and his last employee, Lucas, had become a vampire. Birk couldn't help thinking back to what Mika had said about Lucas being a catalyst. His presence seemed to be everywhere, even though he hadn't been allowed to leave the Ranch in weeks.

Thinking about Mika left Birk confused. They still remembered the way her hand felt and how easily their conversation had flowed. Then there was the pain when she'd walked away after Birk had revealed who they were. They barely knew Mika and didn't understand why the rejection had hurt so much, so they tried to put her out of their mind.

Birk headed upstairs to take off the clothes they had bought to work in—a simple white shirt and jeans now covered in white paint. They had completed a job at Ms.

Broadman's house, where she had held one of her parties last weekend, and Birk needed to scrub themself clean.

The elderly ghoul had been forced to switch from human flesh to animal flesh. The party attendees tended to be horrorphiles who gave slightly less than informed consent for attending the disgusting parties. None of that helped Birk, who knew that the stained walls were a combination of filth that most likely included human blood, no matter what the council said. As long as no one was seriously hurt, they looked the other way.

Birk vigorously scrubbed their body, but they still felt unclean as they put on a flannel shirt and a new pair of jeans. The job may not have been glamorous, but it put some cash in their pocket, allowing them to purchase a few belongings and pay for their food.

By the time they returned downstairs, a few more people had arrived.

It had been nearly a week since Birk had arrived at Rocko's, and they knew that it was time to start making more permanent plans, not that Rocko had ever made them feel less than welcome. But even after they left, this bar would stay a part of them, filling the empty spot from having to leave their sisters. Here, though, they could be themself. All it took was one introduction, and everyone was using their correct name and pronouns, and for the first time, they felt happy or mostly happy.

It had taken Mika three days to show up back at the bar. Birk had stayed as far away from her as possible. When they ignored her, Mika took the hint and didn't try to talk to them again. She returned each day to sit in what Birk had realized was her regular spot.

Birk noticed the alpha heir, Phoenix, hanging out with

the pixies and one of the wolves, the one that always seemed to be around her. Birk couldn't hear the higher-pitched language of the pixies, but they did see the smiles and laughter coming from the wolves.

At one of the tables were the Jamisons, a human couple who frequented the bar at least once a week. One of the men, Jim, raised his hand to say hello, and Birk returned the gesture before sitting down at the counter. They didn't even have to order before slices of veggie pizza appeared in front of them, all because yesterday they had mentioned how much they loved pizza, even if the cheese did not love them back.

"Rocko told me to tell you that this isn't dairy cheese. It is a special vegan kind, so it shouldn't hurt your stomach."

"Thanks, Tim."

Birk looked down at the pizza, their mouth watering in anticipation. The cheese was layered on, causing the mound of chopped vegetables to shift on the top. It may not have been dairy cheese, but it smelled and looked good. They took a big bite, savoring the flavor as they swallowed. Birk was almost ashamed at how much they had looked forward to the human food they could scrounge up before. None of it had tasted like this. Maybe they should have ventured past the dorm cafeteria in college, but they couldn't have known what they were missing. Birk couldn't imagine anyone cooking as well as Rocko.

They had just finished the first slice when someone sat down next to them. They looked up, jolting as their eyes met their mother's. She wore a simple white dress that hung off her body but covered her just enough to be accept-able for going out beyond the forest. Although, in the bar where no one else was dressed up, she stood out.

"You can't possibly be eating that," she said.

"It's so good. You could try a bite."

Birk's mother wrinkled her nose at the pizza and then ignored it. "I came to take you home."

"Really?" Birk realized how loud they were when the entire bar turned to face them.

"It has been long enough for this foolishness. You need to come back with your sisters."

"What do you mean by foolishness?" Birk put the pizza back on the plate, giving it one last longing look before returning their attention to their mother.

"Well, this." Elowen gestured to their flannel shirt and jeans.

The day Birk received their first paycheck, they'd walked over to a thrift store and picked out some new human clothes. The flannel material had felt so soft against their skin, and they hadn't owned a pair of jeans since they had come home from school. They turned around and donated the simple shirt and flowy pants they had arrived in, hoping someone else would find a use for them.

"I like my clothes. I'm not coming back to have you force me into a gender that isn't my own."

"Don't be silly. I'm not forcing anything. You were born my d—, and you will always be my d—. I do not appreciate you trying to kill off J—."

It might have only been a few days since Birk last heard that name, but in that time, they had learned more about who they were than they could have imagined. To hear it now caused their chest to well up with pain and their eyes to water. They were not going to cry in front of their mother, so they stood up. In their new boots, they were slightly taller than their mother, and looked down on her for the first time they could remember.

"I am not. I have never been. If you won't accept that, then you are correct that there is no place back there with my sisters."

Their mother's face twisted in anger, and they spit out, "You will not survive without family."

"You're right," Birk said. "It's a good thing I found one that loves me for who I am."

"Is there a problem here?" Rocko had made his way out of the kitchen and was standing right next to Birk. They had been so focused on their mother that they hadn't noticed him. They hadn't noticed that everyone in the bar was now standing up. The Jamisons had moved right behind Rocko, ready to defend them if necessary. Even the wolves were up, their eyes slightly pinched in anger. Only the pixies were still sitting, disconnected from what was happening.

Birk's mother realized everyone's attention had shifted to them. She let out a shrill scream of frustration, turned, and walked out of the bar.

When the door closed, Birk fell on the stool, the tears falling freely from their face. Rocko reached around them, holding them to his chest, letting them cry. The Jamisons each gave them a pat on their shoulder before going back to their table. The bar settled back in, letting Birk cry in peace. All except for Mika, who was still standing up. When she started to walk toward Birk, they buried their head in Rocko's chest. They couldn't take any more rejection today.

When the tears finally stopped, Rocko used a clean part of his apron to dry off their face.

"I think your pizza has gone cold. It's a good thing I made an entire pie for you."

Birk let out a small chuckle. As Rocko walked back to the kitchen, they looked around the room, thanking everyone with their eyes. When they got to Mika, the woman stared back at them, unmoving, her face closed off. When the new pieces of pizza arrived, Birk finally looked away. She wasn't sure what to do about that woman. Or the realization that her walking away had only hurt so much because some part of them wanted nothing more than to feel her hand in their own again.

B irk was up early the next morning, slipping out the back door of the upper apartment as soon as Rocko had closed the bar. It was still early enough that the streets were mostly devoid of people. Only the coffee shop was open. A lone occupant was visible through the window holding a cup of coffee. Birk remembered him from the bar the night before. The rest of the businesses on the street were closed, and the sidewalk was mostly empty of people. Those who haunted the night were now inside, and all but a few people had yet to wake and leave their houses. Even surrounded by all the buildings, Birk found an echo of the peace they had experienced being near their tree.

Before Birk reached the end of the street, a blue pickup truck pulled over beside them. It was a newer model with a large truck bed, even though it also had a back-row seat.

"Are you ready?" Jim Jamison said as he rolled down his window.

Birk opened the passenger door, pulling themself into the high seat and putting on their seatbelt. "I thought I was meeting you at your house. Am I late?"

"Nope, not at all. I'm early and figured I would save you some walking."

They pulled into the road and Jim started driving out of town.

"I appreciate you taking me today."

"Of course, kiddo. I'm happy to help, and I had to go there for work anyway." The look he gave them was one of sympathy, and Birk wasn't up for it this morning. He may be human and unaware of the entire situation, but unfortunately, that kind of family rejection seemed to cross cultures.

Birk leaned their head against the window, watching the trees go by with a pain that cut deep. They must have nodded off because the drive seemed to last only minutes before they woke to Jim gently prodding their shoulder. Outside, several other trucks surrounded a construction site.

"We're here. Do you know where you need to go?"

Birk shook their head. "I should be able to find it in a phone book."

"A phone book? You really haven't been out all that much, have you?"

Birk opened the door. "Thanks for your help. I should get going."

"Wait a minute. I'm sorry, that was out of line. It's just that it has been years since I saw a phone book lying around. There aren't many pay phones left either. Dave was worried about you and wanted to make sure you could get ahold of someone if there was trouble. We picked this up for you."

Jim reached into one of the cup holders and pulled out a black smartphone. "It isn't anything fancy. The plan is prepaid, so it won't have much data, but it will be good for the next few months. Dave and my numbers are in there, so you can call us if anything happens."

Birk took the phone from him and looked at the screen. They knew about smartphones, even if they had never owned one. It was just that their mother wasn't keen on them having possessions. Besides, there was nowhere to charge a phone in the forest. "Thank you."

"You got money for lunch?"

Birk nodded, too afraid to speak in case their voice broke with the mix of emotion swelling inside them.

"I should be done around three, but if that changes, I'll text you. If you need more time, just let me know."

Birk slipped out of the car at the same moment Jim did. As he headed toward the work site, Birk moved toward the side road. They had never been to Grand Junction before, and the city was overwhelming.

Ember was enough to overwhelm Birk, even though it was a small town. It had been years since they had been anywhere else, not since they had returned from school. This was something else. They started walking along the sidewalk, hoping to find somewhere a little quieter to stop and pull out their phone to try and locate their friend. Cars traveled by at a consistent rate, and each time one drove past, they flinched at the harsh sound and the feel of air hitting their skin.

There was never this much traffic in Ember. As they continued walking, it got worse. There were cars parked back-to-back, letting out children. Some had pulled up to the curb, but others stopped in the middle of the street, doors open and small kids exiting and scampered off toward what looked to be a school. There were children everywhere. Birk thought about crossing the street to escape the chaos, but there wasn't a light nearby, and it seemed impossible to predict when cars would stop or start up again. Instead, they braced themself and walked through the throngs of children. They had never seen so many in one place before. There had to be hundreds all swarming inside the one building.

As they walked past, the tiny bodies brushed them in their haste to catch up with friends or enter the school. They seemed oblivious, walking straight into them, and Birk found themself shuffling around to avoid as many children as they could. When they finally made it past the school, they let out a deep breath but pressed on. They did not want to stop anywhere near that mayhem.

About thirty minutes later, they approached a cafe. It was one of those chain stores they had heard about, but which had not made its way into their town. They entered to find half the tables occupied, but they were relieved to find someplace to sit down.

There was a line to order, but it didn't take long before Birk walked up to the register. The menu was a collection of words they didn't understand, so they decided to stay with the one thing easy enough to order.

"I will take a coffee, please," they told the young female employee in a green apron.

The person behind the register gave Birk a weird look before finally speaking. "What kind?"

"I'll take the regular kind, please."

Birk studied the sign, trying to find a plain coffee. The board was full of complicated names like Cafe Americano and Double Berry Refresher. The gentleman in line behind them cleared his throat loudly, and Birk's cheeks heated.

"How about the dark roast?"

"What size?"

"A small, please."

"We don't have small. You have to order the sizes on the menu."

"Um, I don't know. What size is the smallest?"

The cashier rolled her eyes as she typed into the register. "That will be $2.53."

Birk pulled their cash out of their pocket and handed over a five-dollar bill. They hadn't imagined that a coffee would cost that much.

Once they received their change, they stood there waiting for their drink. The cashier let out a grunt and pointed to a sign at the end of the counter that said "Pick up." Birk sheepishly moved out of the way.

They stood by the pickup counter as employees belted out elaborate coffee orders. They tried to listen to each order, but none of the words sounded like any language they understood. Finally, when the same order had been called three times, the worker, a young man, looked at them.

"Is this yours?"

It was a white paper cup with nothing but the logo of the company on it.

"I don't know."

"Do you have your receipt?"

Birk dug through their pocket, pulling out the dollar bills and sending a scattering of coins to the floor. They took the white piece of paper and handed it to the young man while they picked up the coins. When they straightened, the man was holding the drink and the receipt out toward them, a slight frown on his face.

"It's yours."

"Thank you," Birk said, but the young man had already left to work on another drink.

They took the cup and found an empty table as far in the corner as possible before taking a tentative sip. It was hot and burnt their tongue, so they put it on the table while they pulled out the phone.

On it was a message from Dave, Jim's husband.

"Hope you are finding everything okay. Remember, we are here to help if you need it."

Reading the message brought a sense of peace inside of them. They might have been a disaster at ordering coffee, but they were not a disaster person.

They looked through the screen until they found the internet and typed in the web address to the email provider. Birk pulled up the last email from their friend and copied the address for his company under his name. Then, they put it into the map app. It was going to be a three-and-a-half-hour walk. It was a good thing they had time.

Birk took another sip of their drink. It was bitter and even more unpleasant than beer, if that was possible. They stood up, threw the nearly full cup in the trash, headed outside, and started walking.

B y the time Birk reached the office building, the sun was high in the sky; not quite noon, but not far off. With a start, Birk realized that they could just use their phone to tell the time: 10:43. Technology was pretty fantastic.

The map directions had taken them to a place full of small warehouses with glass storefronts. It was pretty easy to locate the Conservation Conservatory, a vision that Birk's classmate had shared with them back when they were both in school. At the time, he had invited them to join him, but that had been many years ago.

He had reached out a year ago, trying to reconnect and gain a foothold in Ember. Birk just hoped that he was still interested in it.

The door opened with a squeak that echoed through the nearly empty office. There were a few empty chairs in the waiting area and a receptionist at the front of the desk who had been working on her computer before Birk's arrival.

"Hi, I was wondering if Richard Stein is around," Birk said.

"Is he expecting you?"

"No, I'm a friend of his from college. I was in the area and wanted to say hello."

"Who should I tell him is here?"

Birk paused, unwilling … unable … to say the name they had used when they had known each other. "I have a different name now. Can you tell him that his college friend is here?"

"No problem." The woman's voice took on a friendlier tone. "What name and pronouns should I give him?"

Birk blinked back their suddenly watery eyes as they answered, "Birk, and my pronouns are they/them."

The woman walked back to the office, and Birk took a seat in one of the rickety plastic waiting room chairs. It wasn't long before she returned with Richard behind her.

"It has been too long," he said. "You look fantastic. I love the hair and the name."

He reached out and gave them a hug, and it was as if no time had passed. The decades melted away, and they were awkward students once more.

"Let's talk in my office."

As they headed out, Birk turned to the receptionist and gave her a smile. "Thank you."

The woman smiled back and Birk couldn't help but wonder who she had in her life that had made her so accepting, or if she had just always been that way.

"Do you go by Richard now?" Birk asked as they settled into his office. The chairs were a little more padded but still relatively old. It was apparent not much of the company finances went back to furniture.

"Only when I have to pretend to be a businessperson. I still go by Ricky."

"How is Monica doing? You have kids now, right?" Monica had been an English major when they were majoring in environmental sciences. They'd both had the biggest crush on her, but it wasn't until after graduation that Ricky started dating her.

"She is good. Her third book just released. The kids are good as well. Jake just started middle school this year."

"I read her book, well, all of them. She is talented."

"You still wish she liked w—" He stopped himself, pausing briefly before finishing the sentence. "That she wasn't into guys."

"We couldn't have been together anyway."

As if the ice had officially been broken, Ricky leaned forward on his desk and asked, "You left Ember?"

"I haven't left for good. I just came here to visit you."

Ricky didn't know they were a nymph. He had made speculations over the years, and the closest he'd come to the truth had been when he'd accused them of being in a cult.

"Your mom is okay with that?"

"My mom kicked me out. She wasn't very happy with who I am." Birk paused. Those word were still hard to say. Their entire life had been dedicated to their family, and to no longer have that tie, to no longer be able to see their soul, it was still too much to fully process. "You mentioned you were looking into doing some work near Ember. I know it was a while ago, but are you still interested?"

"We haven't been able to make much progress on our current project proposal in that location. We have to take it in front of the town council and, unlike most cities, their sessions are not public. So it has stalled out."

"The project, it isn't anything harmful, right? No new developments or alteration of the landscape?"

"No, nothing like that. I know a project like that wouldn't be accepted there. It is mostly scientific research. They need someone to take some samples and monitor forest growth. I guess there is something unique about the area in which the investor is extremely invested in. Even though I haven't made much progress, the contract is still on the table."

"I need a job."

"Oh." Ricky sat back in his chair, his posture changing, tensing up, falling back on his professional persona. "You haven't done much outside your family since school, have you?"

"No, but what I do for my family isn't that different than what you need for this project. More importantly, I can get in front of the council to get approval. They won't allow an outsider in, especially one who is, well, someone who doesn't have strong ties to the town. I would have to review the proposal, and there may need to be some modifications, but I can get them to at least vote on it."

Ricky sat back in his chair quietly. Birk could almost see his brain thinking, trying to analyze the risk and benefit and trying not to ask questions that he knew they wouldn't answer. Finally, he leaned forward again, his posture relaxing, and Birk let out a sigh of relief.

"Here is what I can do. I can bring you on as a contractor for this project. You will have to sign a non-disclosure agreement until it is ready to be proposed. If it gets accepted, then you will stay with the project. If it doesn't go through, I can only keep you on as long as the investor is willing to pay for you to keep trying to push it through."

"We have a deal." Birk put their hand forward in a fist,

and they both laughed as they did the weird handshake they had developed back in school.

When Birk started the walk back to Jim's construction site, they felt so much lighter. They had a new purpose, one that, after looking briefly through the proposal, they knew would not only be accepted by the council but would also benefit Ember.

The next day, Dave helped Birk set up a bank account at the local branch. The bank was run by the witches, who were equipped to help Birk without copies of their identification. By the afternoon, Birk had given the financial details to her new boss, and the next day, money was deposited into their account, an advance on their salary that was enough to start working on moving out of Rocko's.

Thankfully, Rocko had pointed them toward Old Murray, who had a vacant apartment above his store, the same one Lucas used to live in. It seemed they had walked out of their own life and taken over part of Lucas's. It would have made them sad if they didn't know that he was doing good with his new family.

Birk couldn't help their joy at knowing that they would be at the Ranch in just a few days. They were meeting with the Vampire Mistress, the current head of the council, to convince her to allow Birk to present the project. Lucas would be allowed to attend since it was on their grounds and Birk wasn't at risk.

There wasn't much in the new place—just an old

mattress and a few blankets that must have been left spoiling for a few weeks and had given the room a foul, musty smell. Birk was in the room less than an hour before they packed up their new work laptop and headed back to Rocko's.

It was a busy night, but Birk managed to find a small table to sit at, and Tim brought them a plate of food nearly as soon as they sat down. It was nice to know that Rocko had still been expecting them back.

They opened the laptop and tried navigating to the documents Ricky had sent them for review. It was one thing to occasionally check the library computer but to be carrying one around in their hand left them in awe. Also, thankfully, Rocko's had Wi-Fi because their new apartment did not.

They'd finished their food, a vegetarian pasta dish, and were staring at their screen when they heard the other chair move and felt a person sit down across from them. They looked up, surprised to see Mika.

Birk couldn't help staring. She was so beautiful with her brown eyes and curly chestnut hair. Even the scowl that seemed to be permanently etched on her face didn't take away from the fluttering that went through Birk every time they saw her.

"You got a new computer," Mika said.

"I got a new job. I'm working with a college friend of mine for a project that will be great for Ember."

"I've heard whisperings. You're meeting with the vampires."

Birk suddenly realized how disconnected they had become from the town. Even hidden out with the family, they had always known what was going on. Their place near the council had allowed for that. Now, Mika was still in that position, and Birk was not. But they wouldn't give up who they had become in just this short a time. Besides, if they ever wanted to know anything, they could just ask Rocko.

"I wanted to tell you I am sorry."

"Sorry?" Birk knew exactly what she was apologizing for, but they didn't want to talk about that right now, not after everything good that had happened. They remembered the ease with which the receptionist had used their name and pronouns and wondered why it had been so hard for Mika.

"I don't know if you are aware, but I tend to prefer dating ... well, not men."

"Right."

"Witches, we aren't nymphs. It isn't normal for witch women to have relationships with women or witch men to have relationships with men. My whole life, I have been told that magic can only happen between a man and a woman. I have been struggling with this for a long time, and then you walked in and told me that the whole concept of gender is even more complex, and not binary in the slightest. It was a lot for me to process—not you, not who you are, but how that related to my role in the coven. It is no excuse for walking out like I did."

"You don't have an issue with who I am?"

"Not in the slightest. I think who you are is fantastic, and I should never have made you feel otherwise."

"Thank you for telling me. I know how family can be and how hard it is to be true to yourself while also trying to give them what they want."

Mika smiled a small, sad smile, but even then it was enough to cause Birk to brighten up.

"I heard that you moved above Old Murray's place."

"I did. I have my own apartment."

"You know that is where Lucas used to live."

"It was not only where he used to live but also where he transformed. I have to figure out how to buy a new bed."

Mika raised her eyebrows and tapped the computer screen. "With the magic of the internet, you can get anything. Let me show you."

Birk closed out of the work documents and tilted the computer toward Mika. They scooted their chairs together, and the woman began to show Birk an online world that they couldn't even have begun to imagine.

It had only been three weeks since Birk had been kicked out of their family, and life had started settling into a new routine. They had a bed. It had been delivered in two boxes in the back of a brown truck. When Birk opened one box, a mattress unfolded and then began to expand. In the other box had been a set of metal polls and wooden slats that Birk had stared at in horror before finally turning to their phone and looking at their expanding set of contacts.

Finally, they selected Mika's name and sent her a message.

"Help! The bed came in, and it is all in pieces. I don't know what to do."

Mika arrived thirty minutes later, complete with tools and vegan pizza. It hadn't taken Mika long to make sense of all the pieces and put them together into a platform to hold the mattress. It was like sleeping on a cloud, so much more comfortable than the thin grass of the meadow. Then Mika introduced Birk to a magical site that allowed them to watch movies.

Birk knew what TV was. They had watched plenty of it

while they were away at college, but that had been so long ago and had required a separate device. Birk was realizing that the computer was a tiny box of technological magic. It was even more magical when they laid together on the bed watching.

Things had been going so well that Birk didn't notice they were not feeling well at first. They were a little slower and a little stiff. They had been away from their tree for weeks, but they had gone longer while in school. A little discomfort was to be expected, and they knew they would have to get used to it until they could convince their mother to at least let them visit their tree.

But as Birk walked over to Rocko's for lunch, it took everything they had to keep lifting their legs one step in front of the other. When they entered the door, they sat at the closest table, trying to stop the room from spinning. The pixies started to surround them. They looked at each other and would put their hands on them so slowly that Birk could barely feel the pressure before they let go, and another pixie was there. Soon, Rocko was there, his cold hand on their forehead. They leaned into the chill, enjoying it, but their entire body began to shiver.

"Go get Phoenix." Birk couldn't see who he was talking to. They couldn't see much of anything. Their eyes started to close, but soon, they felt a coarse material covering them. It was followed by more small pieces of fabric as Birk realized that the pixies had all removed their denim vests and piled them on Birk's body.

"I have blankets upstairs," said Rocko. "I'll be right back. Watch over them, please."

Rocko disappeared and Birk let out a small cry, but

soon, they were surrounded by several thinner bodies that leaned against them, holding them up.

They felt blankets covering them, the weight of them not taking away the chill of the day. Something about that didn't seem right to Birk. Fall was still a few weeks away, and the days shouldn't be cold.

They heard the door open and then silence, broken by a voice Birk recognized but couldn't place.

"They say that they are sick, but not their body. Something is eating at their essence. Does that make sense to you?"

It was Phoenix. Birk was happy that they had recognized the voice.

"Something's wrong with their tree. That has to be it."

"Mika," Birk said. They didn't know when Mika had arrived, but they were happy to hear her voice. Soon, they were wrapped up in a pair of slender but firm arms, and Birk felt themself relax and drift off.

Birk woke to darkness. For a brief moment, they thought they had died, until they heard voices.

"There, s— is better now. J—— should be able to hear us and soon will be opening h— eyes."

As if released from a spell, Birk opened their eyes and saw their mother sitting beside them. She held a thin, transparent glass vial, like those they used to store their medicine, in her hands.

"Mommy," Birk whispered and tried to reach out to her, but their arms were still weak.

Their mother stood up and walked over to Rocko, who was hovering next to the kitchen. They were in his apartment, and the space was packed tight. The pixies were there —maybe not all of them, but a few. They flittered around the small room, never moving but always in a new spot. Birk turned away from them before they got an even worse headache than the one they'd had when they'd awoken. Their eyes found Mika. She moved to Birk's side, grabbing and holding their hands tight. The scowl was back on her face, and Birk wanted to do something to change it, but they were still so tired.

"S— isn't cured," Elowen said. "It is just temporary so s — can come to h— senses and return home. Then I will heal h— tree."

"Enough," Mika said as she pulled away from Birk. Birk weakly lifted their hands, trying to catch Mika before she moved, but it was too late. Mika approached their mother. "You will not harm them. You will not poison them, but you also will not misgender them. If you continue to do so, I will bring it before the council."

"S— is my d—. You do not have any jurisdiction."

"They are a magical creature that has been disowned by your family. They fall under the same protection as any family-less creature in Ember. They have rights, and if you continue on this path, you will be tried by the council. Think long and hard about what will happen to your children if you are not around to protect them."

"Is that a threat?"

"It is a promise."

Birk watched as Rocko moved to one side of Mika and Phoenix moved to her other side. They were there standing up to their mother for them.

"Oh, enough of this. You can see I helped, but the tree is mine. It belongs to my land, and I can do what I want with it."

"Mommy, please." Birk tried reaching out again. Their mother's lip curled as she turned toward them.

"I had hoped that you would have learned your lesson and returned to the family."

"This is how you ask them to return?" Mika slid

between Birk and their mother. "Why would they ever want to return to you after you poisoned them?"

"I haven't done anything to them. It is the tree that is sickening. It knows what my child is doing and is merely trying to protect itself. Once Birk comes to h— senses, everything will return to how it is meant to be. H— tree will heal itself, and J— can return to lead the family."

"I may not be a nymph," Rocko's voice echoed off the walls as he spoke, "but I am as much a part of the land as you are. Your trees do not care about human concepts of gender. That is all on you, and what you are doing to Birk's tree is disgusting. Go! get out of my house, and do not return unless you come to bring recompense for what you have done to your offspring."

Elowen puffed up her chest to Rocko to remind him that she would not be taking orders from any man. But he growled, "Go," and she lifted up her skirts and walked out of the room with as much dignity as she could muster.

Mika was at Birk's side in an instant. She touched her hand to their forehead and then trailed it down to their shoulder and arm, as if reassuring herself that Birk was still there. A trail of goosebumps prickled in her wake.

"How are you feeling?" Mika asked.

Birk took stock of themself. Their head still hurt, and their body was still sore. But they were awake, and the room had stopped spinning.

"Better, I think," they said. "What happened?"

"We think your mother has done something to your tree," Rocko said, "but we cannot get close enough to check without violating the treaty and putting the entire magical community's balance at risk. Things improved after Veronica was brought home and the wolves gave up leadership of the council, but this new balance is still so tentative. We have to be careful how we proceed."

"Damn politics," Mika said. "We can go and tell the other nymphs what has happened. To harm a tree for no reason and without restoring balance is bad enough, but to harm one of their own's souls? They must not know what is happening."

"I'm sure they know well enough." Birk moved their hand so it was resting on top of Mika's. "I think you underestimate the hold my mother has over her people. I am sure they not only know, but are actively helping. They believe in my mother, but more importantly, they depend on her."

"We can't just sit by and watch this happen," Mika said.

"No one is suggesting that," Rocko said. "We need to do things in the proper order. Birk is healed for now. I don't know how much longer the remedy will keep them whole, so we should work fast. Mika, you need to go and put a call in to the council; there needs to be an emergency meeting tonight. I will stay with Birk and make sure they are okay."

"I will go as well." Phoenix had stood quietly in the corner of the room, letting things transpire. But now that she was needed, she stepped forward. "Since neither of us officially sits on the council yet, it will be better if we both put forward the call."

Mika's eyes had never left Birk. She clung to their hand desperately, as if afraid to leave.

"I will be okay," Birk said. "You know Rocko wouldn't let anything else happen to me."

"He may not have a choice," Mika said quietly. Then she stood up, letting Birk's hand fall away.

"Let's go do this," she said.

"I'm sorry, I don't have a car," Rocko said. They had set off for the council meeting a few minutes earlier, and Birk was already feeling faint. "I don't go much of anywhere but the bar."

"Where do you sleep? Do you need to sleep?" Birk asked in an attempt to distract themself from their muscles feeling like gelatin. They were not surprised, or even disappointed, when he turned and gave them a smirk instead of answering. The smirk quickly turned into a frown when he saw how much they were struggling.

"I think it's best if I carry you there." He sounded hesitant, as if the thought of holding Birk was something he would rather not do, but he moved over to them and, with their consent, picked them up.

His skin was cold and hard, more like rock than the human flesh it appeared to be. The cold felt good against their skin, and Birk wondered if their fever had not completely broken. They wrapped their arms around Rocko's neck and tried to make themself as easy to carry as possible. Rocko seemed to support them easily, but the journey was full of jostling that did not help Birk's sore muscles.

Rocko put them down on the grass outside the building so that Birk could walk in of their own volition, but their muscles were even more sore after being carried, and their vision swam. They had to reach out and hold on to Rocko.

"I'm good," they managed. They were anything but good, but they moved forward regardless.

The room was already full by the time they arrived. Even the pixies had attended, a first from Birk's recollection. They flitted about the room, some moving from one spot to the next without their movement being seen. Even those who stood in one place seemed to vibrate, causing the area around them to open up, making the room seem even more crowded.

Rocko helped Birk move to a section on the side of the room where there were a handful of chairs for those who needed them. So far, they were empty, but Birk sunk into one gratefully. There was no way they would be able to make it through the meeting standing up.

Birk's mother stared at them, a satisfied leer plastered on her face, before she turned toward the council members.

"Let's get started," Elizabeth said.

Since the Vampire Mistress had taken over as the head of the council for the next decade, they had added a set of stairs leading up to the podium so that the leader of the vampires, who had been transformed at the human age of eight, could be seen.

"This session has been called to address an emergency regarding Birk, formerly of the nymphs, and allegations of poisoning."

"This is ridiculous," Elowen said. "This is a family matter that does not need to be brought before the council."

"Is Birk a member of your family, or have they been cast out?" the werewolf alpha asked.

"I refuse to call them by that ridiculous name."

"Then you agree to end this meeting," Elizabeth said. "We will find in favor of Birk."

"That is not what I said."

"The council has been very clear that members' names, identities, and cultures will be respected," Elizabeth said. "If you choose to disregard that, you will be removed from the council chambers. You may allow someone to speak in your place, or you may forfeit your right to answer to these very serious allegations."

The council room remained silent while the two women battled it out. They stood as if waiting to see what would happen next. Even the pixies were slightly more subdued. They had all moved over toward the wolves, with one wolf, the one Birk recognized as Phoenix's friend, seeming to translate the proceedings in a tone that resonated high above Birk's hearing.

"I will, for the sake of these proceedings, humor my child and will not call my child by the name that they were bestowed upon birth. I do want it on record that the council is not considering my needs. I am a mother grieving the loss of my daughter. To continue to throw that in my face is unnecessarily cruel."

"Your objection has been noted. As head of the council, I have mandated that the precedent set by the previous head of this council shall stand. Respecting an individual's or group's identity will remain the rule of the council unless successfully challenged by a full convening."

There were some gasps in the crowd and some mumbling. A full convening required a trial that continued until every magical family, pack, or collective agreed unanimously on an intended outcome. The last one held had been for the very founding of the treaty that united them.

Birk knew that no matter what happened today, at least the council would continue to be a safe space for them, and they couldn't help the joy that flowed out of them. Vampires were fairly respectful of gender. Having seen gender expectations change over the centuries, they did not hold the same rigid standards developed in the last hundred years. Yet by codifying this right into the treaty, they had made it nearly a certainty moving forward, even in a decade when the vampires gave up the head of the council to the witches.

"Now that, that is settled," Elizabeth said. "Will you please do the council the favor of answering the alpha's question? Is Birk, the individual sitting right there, a part of your family?"

"The person in question is no longer a nymph. Not unless they renounce their wild claims and choose to embrace what makes them the person they were meant to be."

"I will no longer accept evasion on your part," Elizabeth's voice spit out in a high-pitched yowl that caused Birk to shiver in unexpected fear. "I did not ask if you considered them a nymph. That is not what is up for discussion today. Answer plainly. Are they currently a part of your family, or are they not?"

"They are not."

"Now, we may move on to the charges. You have been

accused of poisoning your child by proxy. What do you have to say for yourself?"

"I have not laid a hand on my child. The only thing I have done is provide a remedy to help relieve symptoms. I cannot help it if the tree is rejecting them based upon their rejection of their identity."

"That is ridiculous," Mika said loudly enough for the whole room to hear. "We all can figure out that you are the one poisoning the tree to get them back under your control."

"That is enough. There will be time for witnesses to come forth later," Elizabeth said.

Birk strained to see Mika. She was standing with the witches in the back of the room. Her face was turned toward the council table, and Birk couldn't help the pang of sadness that they were not together, even though they knew her place was with her coven.

"Do you have anything else to add?" Elizabeth asked.

"There is nothing more to be said," Elowen said.

"Then who first connected this sickness to their tree?"

One of the pixies moved to the front of the council room, right underneath the table. The entire swarm followed. All of them buzzed around, though most of those present couldn't hear the flutter of their wings.

"Excuse me." The same male wolf moved forward. Phoenix remembered seeing him a few times at Rocko's. "The pixies were the ones who first noticed. If it would be alright, I can translate for them."

"Go ahead, Ancil."

The pixies started to move faster, and the young wolf's brow creased as he tried to catch everything they said. If they talked as fast as they moved, Birk could only imagine what he was listening to.

"They said that they noticed there was a sickness in Birk's essence. They could sense the presence of an attack and saw that it was eating away at Birk's inside. They are very concerned because the medicine may give the physical shell strength, but it does nothing to heal the inside. That is still getting darker." Ancil turned away from the pixies, looking up at the council. "I'm sorry. You know that isn't an exact translation. The pixies think in terms different than our own."

"Do any species able to communicate with this group have any objections to the translation being entered in as record?"

Elizabeth paused long enough for someone to come forward. When no one did, she continued. "Does anyone else have anything further to add?"

"I do," Mika said.

"I trust you will keep your emotions under control this time?"

"I will. I was present during the interaction where Elowen provided a remedy to Birk. The elder nymph claimed that it was the tree that was making Birk sick, but she mentioned briefly that it was happening with her aid. I do not believe that she thought anyone heard her as she said it, but I did."

"That is outrageous," Elowen said.

"As accused, you were allowed to speak first and will speak last, as is our way. For now, you will let others speak. Can anyone attest to the connection of a nymph to their tree?"

"I can, at least the little that I know."

"Rocko, nice to see you finally decided to attend a meeting. Please, continue."

"As you all know, I am not from Ember. I grew up across the country in another nexus, a small one that is held by the trolls. Like the nymphs, we have a connection to nature. I am a rock troll. While I may be male, rocks themselves do not have any gender. Trees are also a part of nature. It would not make sense for them to follow human gender roles. I have never met another nymph family. They tend to keep to themselves, sequestered as far away from others as they can. Most families are not as large as the one here in Ember. But my mother told me stories, and they contained nymphs of all genders."

Birk shot up at that. It was more than he had told them earlier. They understood why he wouldn't have said more. It was just secondhand information, but to know of other families, even if it were rumors, was more than Birk could imagine. A sinking feeling settled in their gut. It had been their job to liaise with the other families, but if what Rocko had said was true, then it was no wonder that their mother had never let them do so. They turned and glared at Elowen, but she just looked back, unfazed.

"That is interesting," Elizabeth said. "We value the wisdom that has been passed down to us orally from our ancestors, but we cannot solely make our decision based upon secondhand accounts. Birk, please tell us your side of things."

Birk tried to stand, but their body was still weak, and they found that they couldn't lift themself properly out of the chair.

"You may remain sitting. Please tell us when you knew that you were not female."

"When I was younger," Birk started, uncertain, as they had never said these words out loud. "I always knew I was different from my sisters, but I didn't know how. It wasn't until I went off to school that I understood there were different genders. Even then, I was so busy trying to understand this new world that I had been thrust into that I didn't have time to sit and explore who I was. But when I returned, I saw that the world was more than what my mother had said it was. It took some time for me to examine these new facts. I talked to some people who helped me know what to look up. Maybe if I was a man, I would have known earlier, but to be neither male nor female, to be without gender—that isn't talked about and it took me longer to understand. I know I have always been this way. Being able to say it, being able to adjust who I am to better represent who I am inside, doesn't mean that I am not the same kid who planted my soul and watched it grow. My tree never rejected me—my mother did. I know that because my tree knew before my mother, and handled it just fine."

"Very well. Elowen, do you have anything else to say?"

"Yes. You use the treaty to justify what is happening here today, so let me do so as well. The land where our soul trees live is sacred. The treaty specifies that the sacred land of a family is to be governed by that family. Birk, as you call them, has been exiled from the family. It is my right, and my obligation, to protect our land from contaminated human ideas. Even if you claim that the tree is their soul, which I contest, the land it sits on is ours. What happens to that land is, by the rights of the treaty, mine to manage."

The council room was loud, with all attendees talking while waiting for the decision. The council members had left the room to deliberate on the matter at hand. It wasn't unprecedented, but it also wasn't something that happened often. Usually, matters were discussed openly in front of the community for all to hear. Only the most complicated or sensitive of matters were finalized behind closed doors. Birk couldn't help but wonder which one their situation fell under.

They stared at the stage with the now empty table and chairs. It was easier than looking around and finding people gaping at them while they were gossiping, or worse, to see their mother, who had not stopped glaring at them. Even now, Birk felt her stare.

The council had been gone for over an hour, and Birk had been alone most of the time. Rocko had sat with them at first, but then he was called into the council chambers. He had yet to return.

Birk had hoped that Mika would join them, but she had stayed huddled in the back of the room with the other witches. It hurt at first, but Mika was in a difficult situation. She had at least stood up for them when it counted. They couldn't ask for anything more.

They tried not to sink into the hopelessness that came when you were rejected by your own kin, the people who were supposed to stay by your side no matter what. If they didn't love you, then who would? But that led to dangerous thinking. They knew that they would build their own family in time. They had already started.

Birk dared to look up, making a point to ignore their mother. The room was full of people who had come to hear and bear testimony to what was happening to them. It was enough for now, and it was more than they'd had before. Even if they had to walk this path alone, at least they would walk it as their true self.

The door in the back of the stage that led to the council chamber opened. Rocko walked out, an unreadable expression on his face. He lumbered off the stage and toward Birk, glancing at them before positioning himself behind them.

"What happened?" Birk asked.

Rocko just shook his head slightly and continued his intense focus on the empty stage.

It was not empty for long. Elizabeth walked onto the stage first. Instead of going to the podium, she settled into her seat at the table.

The other members followed behind her. There were ten in total. The vampires, werewolves, and witches each held a permanent seat. Five others were headed by other large magical communities that had changed over the years. Elowen had once held a seat, right after first becoming matron of the family. She had lost it just a few years later. No one would tell Birk why. The ninth seat rotated amongst the smaller families and was currently being held by a brownie. The last seat represented all of the solo magical beings, of which Birk was now a part. The seat was elected every year and was currently being held by a mouse shifter. She was quiet and fidgety, but Birk realized it was probably time to get to know her.

Elizabeth gave Birk a glance of sympathy before she turned her head and focused on the room, once again a neutral expression on her face. Birk studied the rest of the council members. They looked somber, all except for the witch council member who represented in Mika's stead. He looked downright joyous. It was not a great sign, and Birk clenched their hands on the chair, preparing for the worst but not knowing what that would be.

"Let's come back to order," Elizabeth said. The room had already gone quiet, filled with anticipation when the council members arrived.

"The treaty is an important document that unites us when nothing else would. You all know that Ember was the first nexus to be controlled by multiple magical species. Things have not always gone smoothly, but with everyone respecting the treaty, we have ultimately remained at peace. I say that so you know that our ruling was not made lightly. What happens here today will impact our community for generations. Ultimately, the treaty must be upheld.

"Elowen is correct that the treaty is clear that a family's land belongs to them. They are allowed to dictate this use. I was here when this section was written, as some of you were as well. We knew that we would have diversity. We value different things, and those differences are not to be judged by others as long as they do not threaten our identity with the humans. If the nymphs choose to poison their land, that is their choice, and the council will not intervene."

The room erupted in chatter. Birk heard Mika's scream of frustration in the back of the room.

"However," Elizabeth said. When the room did not quiet, she tried again, louder. "However."

The room was still in an uproar, no one listening, and Elizabeth's voice was unable to break through it.

"The vampire is speaking. You will all stop now." The werewolf alpha's voice boomed through the crowd. The room, used to him as head of the council, quieted instantly.

"Thank you," Elizabeth said. "Now, as I was saying. It is also true that we must protect members of the magical community. Each member of a group is the responsibility of the head of their group. Over the years, magical individuals have wandered in without their own community, and the treaty was updated with special provisions for their care. As Birk is no longer part of the nymph family, they fall under these provisions.

"The treaty is very clear that individual members are to be protected by all members of the magical community. No harm may come to them while they are residents or within the city boundary of Ember. Birk has lived here their whole life. They qualified instantly as an individual member when they were forced out of their family."

"Like you would have done any differently," Elowen said.

Elizabeth ignored her outburst and continued. "The council cannot tell you to stop poisoning your land, but you are responsible for Birk's well-being. You will supply them with medication that is the appropriate dosage to keep them well as often as it is needed. Failure to do so will bring your entire family charges from the council."

A low growl came from Phoenix, but the alpha gave her a glance that immediately silenced her. That didn't stop others from murmuring their dissatisfaction, and through it all, Mika's voice rang out.

"You can't do that. That isn't good enough. The medicine is barely sufficient to keep them alive. You see them over there. They don't even have the strength to stand."

"I made that case," Rocko said. He looked even more upset than when he had left the room.

Tension filled the room. It hadn't been that long since the council was on the verge of dissolving, and the vampires had been preparing for war. Things were still so tenuous. Birk knew that if they didn't do something, the tension would build, and the consequences would extend far beyond themself. They didn't want that to happen.

They held on to the chair arms and attempted to stand. Their arms and legs still felt wobbly, and they weren't sure they were going to be successful, but strong arms wrapped around them, supporting them.

"I understand that the council has to think about all members of Ember." Their voice came out quieter than they expected, and they tried to speak up. "I will never condone the harm being caused to my tree, but I will abide by the council's decision."

They didn't sit down, so much as collapse as Rocko helped them down. They leaned their head back on the chair and let out a brief sigh. They didn't know that a body could hurt so much. They couldn't remember ever being sick before. As long as their tree was whole, they were whole. Only now, their tree was in danger.

"That brings us to our last point," Elizabeth said. "This is not as clear-cut as the other two points, as it is particular to nymph customs. We need a few areas clarified. Elowen, is it accurate that the soul-bonded tree is unique to a specific nymph and that within your family, no other members, not even the mother of the child, will then touch the tree once it has been planted?"

"It is true that no one will touch another nymph's soul, but that … that … person sitting there is no longer a nymph."

"The council is not here to debate Birk's specific identification. They have been identified as a nymph since their birth, and the council does not see your bigotry as justification to seek reclassification."

"How dare you."

"How dare I? I am the mistress of the night. I have wandered about these lands since long before you were born. In the interest of our community, I am playing within the rules, but just so we are clear, I know more about your people than you have forgotten. Rocko may not have been able to give direct testimony about other families, but I did. This council has heard how you have twisted your community to your self-interests and how the treaty protected you enough to do so, but if you keep interrupting me, I will explain to the entire room what started your drive for a female-only family. Then, I will go to the rest of the nymphs and tell them that you have been making them kill their sons because of your hate. Will you shut up now?"

Elowen's face contorted in pure loathing directed at the vampire, but she didn't utter a word.

Birk's mind swam with everything that had been said. The faces of the three infants that had been sent to the river during their lifetime filled their mind. None of it had needed to happen, and other people had known the entire time. Birk had cried each time they had held the ceremony, a ceremony that apparently didn't even exist in other families. Each time, their mother had told them how defective the children were. How what the nymphs were doing was merciful. It took them a moment to catch back up with Elizabeth's words.

"The council has found that the land the soul trees are planted on may belong to the nymph family, but the tree itself belongs to the individual. No other being may touch the tree without the nymph's direct permission. If this is found to be violated, then the entire nymph family will be brought before the council on charges. And just to be clear, Birk's classification as a nymph is not under question. If you wish to dispute this status, then you can put in a request to speak to me, and I will determine if and when it will be added to a regularly scheduled session. That is all. You can all go home now."

Despite Elizabeth's invitation to leave, the only person who left immediately was Elowen. Birk was happy to see their mother go. The rest of the room sat around talking in groups. There were mutterings about what this would mean for the rest of the magical community, as well as what this meant specifically for Birk, but Birk didn't want to hear any of it. They even ignored Rocko, who stood behind them patiently as they kept their head down, waiting for the room to clear out.

Finally, Birk looked up to see only Rocko and Mika. As if waiting for this moment, Mika immediately started talking.

"There has to be some way to appeal. There is no way

they can expect you to live like this. It isn't right that the council thinks this is an acceptable solution."

Birk couldn't help it and started to laugh.

"It's not funny."

"Don't you see?" Birk asked. "Elizabeth told me everything I needed to know to fix this situation. I mean, it isn't going to be easy, but it should be doable."

Birk looked at both Rocko and Mika, and when they realized that the two did not understand, they couldn't help it—they laughed again, until their body reminded them why that was not a great idea.

Rocko and Mika had decided that Birk should not be left alone and moved them back to Rocko's room. Birk did not resist, the small room felt more like a home than their new place had yet to become. It was also nice to have people fussing over them. Besides, they were unable to move without assistance, and that would have left them trapped in a room far away from the people they now called family.

They had Birk situated in the bed, sitting up with pillows that had not been there earlier, to help support them. Rocko had given them a vial of medicine that Elowen had reluctantly handed him, but it did little more than take the edge off the soreness spreading throughout their body.

"Do you plan on revealing what the rest of us missed?" Mika asked.

The words came out brusquely, but Birk caught the concern and underlying fear for them, and it warmed Birk despite their lingering chill. Oh, Birk had been with lovers of all genders. Most of them had been human, and there had always been a barrier between who Birk was and who they thought Birk was. With Mika, the barrier had been torn down. Birk lifted their hand slightly, and Mika sat on the edge of the bed and put it in her own.

"They declared that the tree is mine, so all we have to do is move it."

"Move an adult tree?" Rocko asked. He was seated at the small table, his frame threatening to break the chair beneath him.

"It can be done," Birk said. "It isn't ideal, but it is better for my tree than to stay in direct harm. It helps that I am still relatively young. Even a normal tree would have a chance of survival, but my tree is linked to me. We will pull through together."

"How?" Mika asked. "You heard what the council said. The land belongs to the nymphs, and we won't have permission to even approach the tree."

Rocko let out a low laugh that shook the floor of the room. "Clever," he said. "That vampire must really like you."

Mika looked between Rocko and Birk. She had her trademark scowl on her face, and Birk couldn't help their smile. Finally, they decided to clue the witch in on what Rocko had figured out.

"Elizabeth made it very clear the land belongs to all nymphs. She also made a point of clarifying my status as a nymph. Therefore, I have the same ancestral rights as the rest of the family. My mother may be able to act in what she determines is the land's best interest, but she cannot deny me entrance anymore. It should be enough to allow a group of people to come help me move my tree to a new home. If I read the vampire correctly, she will assist us long enough for us to finish. At that point, if I lose access to the land, it won't matter. If my tree is not there, then that land is no longer connected to me anyway."

"It still doesn't explain how we get the help to move a tree," Mika said.

"I have an idea about that. Do you, by chance, have any clue where my phone is?"

Mika stood up and grabbed Birk's phone, where she must have plugged it in to charge after Birk had passed out. It may have been a small thing, but it let Birk know that Mika was looking out for them. Now, if only they could get better so they could help Mika out in return.

"Thank you," Birk said as they took the phone and selected their contact list. A few new phone numbers had been added to their contacts. They now had Phoenix, and to Birk's surprise, there was a contact labeled "The Pixie Hive." Birk scrolled down to Ricky's number and hit "dial."

"Where have you been?" Ricky's voice escaped out of the phone, and Birk put it on speaker. "I have been trying to call you for hours. You did it. Not that I didn't trust you, but I didn't expect it to happen so fast."

Birk looked at Mika and Rocko in confusion, but they seemed just as lost as Birk.

"What do you mean?" Birk asked.

"I got a call from the head of the council, an Elizabeth Smith, letting me know that the project was approved. There were a few modifications, as you suggested, but the funder immediately agreed. We are ready to move on to the next steps."

"Oh, that is great to hear."

"You sound surprised," Ricky said.

"Did you talk to Elizabeth already?" Mika spoke quietly so that it would not pick up on the phone.

Birk shook their head and went to shrug their shoulders, but it started the room spinning.

"I just didn't expect her to contact you directly, or so soon, that is all. If you haven't already, can you send over the updated project scope?"

"It's already in your email. What is wrong? You don't sound so good."

"I'm a bit under the weather, but I'm taking care of it. It is actually why I called. I need some help moving a tree."

"Is this the tree Elizabeth mentioned?" Birk stared wide-eyed at their friends.

"Can you tell me what exactly Elizabeth told you about the tree?" Birk asked.

"Part of the revision to the project scope was that five acres of land would need to be purchased by the funder and that land would be held for use by the project manager, which is only allowed to be you. If the funder backed out of the project or positioned for a new project manager to the council, the land would be gifted to you. Part of that clause included the relocation of a mature birch tree that would be selected by yourself. It seemed like a weird request, but the funder mentioned that he thought it was a family matter and it was best to agree to the terms."

"Who exactly is this funder?" Mika asked.

"Who is there with you?"

"These are my friends. They are helping take care of me."

"They know about your family?"

"They know the stuff I can't tell you."

"And this tree, it has something to do with your mother?"

"The tree has everything to do with me. However, why

it needs to be moved has to do with my mother. It needs to be relocated off of our ancestral land."

"This Elizabeth person stuck up for you. I am glad you have people like that in your corner."

"I am too." Birk looked at Mika and Rocko as they spoke. "However, I think Elizabeth's intervention has more to do with her history with my mother than anything to do with me."

"I guess all that matters is it worked out in your favor. So, what is the plan for this tree?"

Once Ricky had agreed to help, Birk was ready to go save their tree then and there. The thought of it trapped with their mother, being poisoned, was too much. Especially when they had the power to stop it. But Mika had reminded them there were still things that needed to be done behind the scenes, stuff they could not help with, so they reluctantly stayed in bed until they drifted off to sleep, their dreams full of their tree.

When Birk woke, the room was quiet. Even the murmuring of the bar below was hushed. Birk jolted up, afraid something was very wrong, but their head began to hurt, and the room spun around.

"It's okay," Rocko said. Birk soon felt his cool hands on their forehead. "It is time for another dose."

"What time is it?" Birk asked.

"It's midmorning."

"I didn't mean to sleep that long. We should go. Has Ricky arrived?"

"It was suggested that we wait until nightfall. That way,

more of your people will be sleeping, and the vampires will be able to back us up if needed."

Birk took the vial Rocko handed them and drank it down in one gulp. It tasted like dirt and seaweed. Birk realized that it was the heal-all tonic that their mother had given them any time they were sick or had hurt themself as a child. Although admittedly, it must be doing something if they were well enough to notice what they had not before.

The afternoon was a long, painful one for Birk. They had finally convinced Rocko to let them leave the room, and he had helped them shower and dress before settling them at a table in the bar. Only the pixies approached them. They flitted around, occasionally touching a part of them, as if reassuring themself Birk was still whole. Everyone else stayed away, although there were plenty of whispers, even amongst the humans. When Mika arrived, Birk was relieved, both for seeing the woman and for the way it eased their nervous energy.

"How much longer?" Birk asked.

"It's time to go," Mika said.

Birk sat in the passenger seat of Mika's car. It was a red four-door hatchback that had been scrubbed clean inside and out. It even smelled new, like Mika had rarely driven it, which was probably the case. There was a lot in Ember that you could walk to, especially for the witches who tended to live in the town amongst the humans.

The ride seemed to take forever, even though it couldn't have been more than ten minutes before they pulled up in the parking area in front of the forest. Ricky was waiting for them with a conservatory truck and a flatbed that would carry the tree to the new location.

The lights of his truck bore down on the darkness of the

forest, and Birk knew that somewhere in there, their sisters were waiting. It didn't hit them until that moment how much they missed them. As if sensing Birk's emotions, Mika reached out and put her hand on Birk's, holding it gently.

"Are you ready?" Mika asked.

Birk gave a slight nod and then opened their door.

"Thank you for coming," Birk said.

Ricky looked at the forest in awe. "This is where you grew up? Here in these trees?"

"It explains a lot, doesn't it?"

"Not everything, but yes, it explains quite a bit. What is the plan?"

"I think maybe I should go in first and make sure the path is clear."

"Do you expect any problems? If we need to, I can bring out some of my people. I was just told to come with as little help as possible. You got me and the two guys over in the flatbed."

"Fewer people are good in case there are complications. There may be challenges about who is allowed on the land."

"We might as well face them together," Mika said.

As they walked toward the forest, a path began to open, and Birk felt the land welcoming them. They had only made it past the first layer of trees before someone stepped into their path.

"Mother," Birk said.

"Mother?" Ricky questioned.

Elowen had completely forgone clothing and stood naked, her body only visible from the moonlight spilling through the treetops. Birk tried to imagine what the scene might look like to a human. Elowen appeared no older than Birk did themself, although they possessed a gracefulness and authority Birk knew they lacked.

"We are here for my tree," Birk said.

"You cannot be here. This is my people's land, and you are no longer one of us." The lackluster light of the half-moon shone on Elowen, giving her a slightly haunted look.

"Per the treaty, this land belongs to all nymphs. If you want to attempt to change my records, then go ahead and try, but until that time, I have access to the land and can invite others in as needed. If you block me access, I will go to the council. They will let me in."

"If you last that long," Elowen said.

Her face was so full of hate and anger that it had lost its natural beauty. Birk almost found themself feeling sorry for her, but then they remembered all the unnecessary pain she had caused their family. "Elizabeth is waiting for our call. We could have the meeting tonight and I will be back here to get my tree as the sun rises. Not only will I last that long, I think I would prefer it. At least that way I could find out why you became so hurtful."

Elowen stood unmoving, keeping the path blocked but not pressing the issue, as if thinking over her options. Finally, she spoke. "I may have to give you access, but I do not have to let others in."

"It didn't have to come to this," Mika said. "It is one thing to exile your only child, but to try and kill them? No one in this community will stand for that."

"They have, though," Birk said. "They let you for years and years, all those sons that you fed to the river that could have grown up here."

"Enough," Elowen said. "You may go to your tree. Your

friends must stay. Sister Woodruff, you may provide escort. Make sure that s— doesn't touch anything except h— tree."

"You were told to stop misgendering them," Mika said.

"I was told that I had to use those fowl terms in the council chamber. We are here in my forest, and I will call my d— by h— proper name and gender."

Birk looked up to Mika, caught between protecting their friends from their mother or going to see their tree. It had been so long, and the pull was strong, even more so now they were closer.

"Go," Mika said. "Elizabeth and the council members will come. See your tree. Save it. I will protect the human until the council arrives, and we will follow you."

Birk followed Sister Woodruff down the dirt path away from their friends. The forest seemed to close behind them, making it impossible to see Mika and Ricky, even though Birk kept looking back to try. After a minute, the pull of their tree became too much, and they could focus on nothing but moving forward. The forest was dark, with just the highlights of the moon coming through the branches, but Birk was a nymph and had lived most of their life in the forest. It was more like coming home than anything.

Nymphs did not have extraordinary night vision like the wolves or vampires, but they were connected to the land around them in a way that others could not understand. It was another sense that helped to guide them, and having been gone so long from the land, Birk felt it all the stronger. They no longer took it for granted, especially knowing this was most likely the last time they would step foot in this forest.

"I heard what you said," Sister Woodruff said.

The sound broke into the night, bringing Birk back to the moment.

"What did I say?"

"The babies, the ones fed to the river."

"Did you know that nymphs don't have to be female? All that time you didn't tell my mother who I was, did you know?"

They walked in silence, Birk waiting for an answer. The forest seemed to extend the path, as if willing this conversation to continue.

"Your mother is nearing two hundred years old. She is one of the oldest of our family, inheriting it from her mother. However, she is not the oldest. I was born just a few years before her. We were raised together as sisters."

Birk stopped walking, the realization hitting them at once. "You knew?"

Sister Woodruff stopped as well. They were on a footpath in between other sisters' trees. Both stood straight to not touch what belonged to another.

"Your mother waited as long as she could to have you. She needed an heir, someone to maintain the connection to the land. She couldn't stand the thought of lying with a man, so she went to a doctor's office and made sure that you were to be born female, but she never really understood. Your mother was not very nurturing, as you know, and you spent most of your youth with me. When you were young, I would tell you stories, fairytales told to me when I was growing up. You would play out all the roles, and even then, I knew you were not the daughter your mother wanted."

"When I asked you to call me by my new name, you never questioned because you already knew? I thought you were afraid to talk about it."

"There were others like you when I was growing up. Things were different before your mother took charge."

"How could you let this happen?" Birk wanted to shout it out to the forest, but their voice came out small and weak.

"Do you remember when I went away? It was after your mother started training you. I missed having a child around, and I decided to finally have one of my own. I was afraid before, but the call became too much after raising you."

"You left, but you came back alone."

"I told your mother that it didn't work and that I must be unable to have children. But I had a son. I couldn't bring him back knowing what would happen."

"Where is he?" Birk was afraid of the answer, but at the same time, they needed to know if they had a brother out there somewhere in the world.

"There is a small family up north in Montana. They had heard rumors about what had happened to our family. That is why they do not visit us. They are scared of what would happen. We live in the nexus with the largest family left on this continent. What if your mother's ideas spread?"

"Why did you come back?

"For you and him. I missed you, and I knew that if I did not come back, she would come looking for me and find him. I could handle what she would have done to me and my tree, but not what she would have done to him."

"What about the others that she sent to the river?"

"They were all adopted by other families. The mermaids revere children, as you know. They would have never let anything happen to them, and they helped me get them to safety until I could find new homes for them."

"All this time." Grief and anger swirled around inside of Birk. "Why didn't you stop her?"

"It's her family. One day, it will be yours. She will not have another heir. You can move your tree, but when the time comes, it will be your turn to heal what she broke."

"Why? How could she have done this?"

"When she was younger, she was hurt. No, it doesn't justify all the hurt she put onto others, or onto you, but the pain was real. It is her story to tell, and maybe one day she will. But until then, know that she had her reasons. They were shortsighted and full of pain, but in her head, they were necessary. Now, I think it is about time that we reached your tree. I am sorry I could not do more to protect it. It was forbidden."

They started walking again, and almost immediately, the path led up to Birk's tree. The base was entirely covered in salt. Birk collapsed to the ground and began shoveling it off, trying not to put it on another tree in the process. The salt had been laid down inches thick, a slow poison that was leaching the life from the birch. It would have killed their tree in a matter of months, but some part of them was happy that it was not something else, something irreversible.

By the time Mika, Ricky, and the rest of the council arrived, Birk had managed to clear off about half of the ground. Mika and Ricky immediately dropped down to help. When Elowen protested, Birk heard Elizabeth give a curt "enough," causing their mother to fall silent. But Birk's focus remained on their tree, their mind still processing the conversation.

"It's okay," Ricky said. He pulled Birk's hands away from the ground. They were raw from digging the dirt around the rough texture of the bark and stung from the salt. "I have something that will help get the rest of the roots clear."

Birk rose, looking at the mess that was their tree. It had been a month since they had left their home, but the salt had already started taking a toll. To see it so sickly tore at Birk, and to know that their mother had done it was too much. She was still there, watching over the process, anger twisting her face. Elizabeth stood in front of her, as if blocking her off completely.

Ricky pulled out what looked like a long metal pipe that was hooked up to a compressor they had carried in. There was a nozzle at the end that pushed out air, removing the dirt and salt and uncovering the roots that had started shriveling up from lack of nutrients.

The root system of Birk's tree was not substantially large compared to trees that spread out for miles. It was enough to give it stability and nutrients in the Colorado forest. But uncovering it took a few hours as Birk stood by helpless, wishing they could hold on to Mika but understanding why the witch needed to keep her distance in front of the council.

"I'm going to need to go back to bring some supports," Ricky said into the silence of the night.

"That won't be necessary," Rocko said.

He went up to the tree, stabilizing it at the base as Ricky finished excavating the roots. When the tree was safely out, Rocko balanced it on his shoulder and started walking toward the flatbed truck like he was carrying planks of wood and not an entire tree.

Ricky looked in fear, his face frozen, then he glanced around at the assembled group and kept his mouth shut, following the rock troll. Birk knew there would be questions later when they were in a safer location.

"There, your tree is gone," Elowen spat. "Now get out of my home."

The council members disappeared, some walking out of the forest and others blending into the night. Birk turned to Sister Woodruff. "You could come with me. We could move your tree, too."

"My place is here. However, do not be surprised if I turn up for a visit."

"I would like that."

Birk reached in and hugged their adoptive mother, wishing that things could be different, but knowing that everyone had their own choices to make. Once everyone else left, Birk looked at Mika and took her hand in their own. Together, they walked away, and Birk couldn't help wondering if Sister Woodruff was right, if they really would be back here one day leading their sisters—their family.

Lights hanging from the porch of the roof left a white glow on the yard. In the area directly surrounding their tree, they had put up battery-operated torches to keep flame away from their soul, which illuminated the tables full of food. In the center was their tree. It had been a month since it had been moved, and it had handled the transition spectacularly well, thanks to Ricky's noninvasive measures and a bit of nymph magic.

It was the first night of fall. The air was crisp, lacking summer's heat. The birch would soon lose its leaves and go into dormancy, but it was all a part of the cycle of the seasons. It was not an ending or even a pause, just a different time of life.

Birk felt blessed to see their chosen family moving around the tables, talking and eating with each other. Rocko had brought the new bartender, who was talking with Lucas and Jeffery. Lucas had been given a special pass to leave the Ranch. It probably helped that Elizabeth herself was here. Even Sister Woodruff had shown up. She was flirting wildly with Ricky in front of his wife. Both of them would break into laughter whenever he flushed red.

Ricky hadn't pushed too hard when Birk had told them there were things he wasn't allowed to know about, things it was *best* he didn't know about. They had given him the same line in college, but now he seemed to believe it. When Birk had invited him, he had asked if the child from the tree was going to be there, with the suggestion that his children would have someone else to play with. Birk had mentioned the possibility that Elizabeth was actually the oldest of the group. When the couple had arrived, they'd let Birk know that their kids had decided to stay with a babysitter.

Birk reached down and picked up a handful of the soil, letting it drift through their fingers. The land was starting to transform. They had become more and more connected to each other as the days had gone by. Birk could even picture other trees joining their own, someday.

For now, Birk had their work. Some part of them wondered who was behind the grant, which was essentially a study on the impact of ley lines and the congregation of magical communities on the land. But all the data they turned in was scientific, lacking anything in the magical. It was a good study, one they were happy to dedicate their time to.

They turned and saw Mika leaning against the porch railing of the house that had happened to be built on the plot of land given to Birk's care. The deed, made out in their name, had been left on the kitchen table. The house looked like it had been built more than a century ago and was well maintained, but it was not near as beautiful as the woman standing in front of it.

Birk walked over to Mika and took her hand, helping to

guide her down the steps. She was wearing a bright purple skirt that twirled with each step, and Birk couldn't keep their eyes away. They led her toward their tree.

"I heard that you enjoyed dancing with beautiful women," Birk said.

"Not just women," Mika said. "Gender is a spectrum, after all."

"Oh yeah?" Birk said.

Music started to drift from one of the tables, and Birk let a smile grow on their face.

"Would you do me the honor of dancing with me?" Birk asked.

The two held on to each other, swaying gently to the music, neither caring that Birk didn't know how to dance.

"I will do more than dance with you," Mika said.

Birk hitched their eyebrow as they stared into beautiful brown eyes. "What do you mean?"

"Well, let's start with a date and see where it goes from there."

"What about your coven?"

"I think it is time that I educated them about the complexities of gender."

Birk leaned in until their lips connected. Birk's hands clenched the back of Mika's shirt as their body raged with want. Mika's hands went to Birk's neck, pulling them closer.

Someone let out a loud whistle, and Birk suddenly remembered the yard full of people. They pulled back, but only partly, but their bodies were still connected, and they continued to dance beneath the silver birch, whose branches nodded occasionally, as if in approval.

Get a FREE Short Story!

Join My Newsletter

Sign up at mj-james.com

Continue the Ember Town Series with Mika!

Visit mj-james.com to order

ACKNOWLEDGMENTS

Thank you. Writing is hard work, but it is even harder to connect your book with readers. Whether Birk is your first book of mine, if you started your journey with Lucas, or if you have read everything I have written - I appreciate you. I could not keep writing without readers like you.

Each time I write an acknowledgment, I sit in wonder at how far we have come from my debut book, In-Between. I cannot help but think about how thrilled my younger self would have been. I was the kid who always had a notebook and pen in my hands and a paperback book in my back pocket. I can't help but think how much my younger self desperately needed to see themselves in the books that they read.

I am so incredibly grateful to the amazing people who help me with my writing. Thank you to my beta readers, Lilian and Tessy, for helping me make this book the best it can be. While I do not promise perfection, this book could not be as polished without my editor, Rebecca Scharpf. Also, Skye Alley, who gives voice to my characters, I am extremely grateful to keep working with you.

www.ingramcontent.com/pod-product-compliance
Lightning Source LLC
Chambersburg PA
CBHW070516200726
48293CB00007B/2565